NURSE IN DANGER

NURSE IN DANGER

Jane Converse

CHIVERS
THORNDIKE

This Large Print book is published by BBC Audiobooks Ltd, Bath, England and by Thorndike Press®, Waterville, Maine, USA.

Published in 2006 in the U.K. by arrangement with the Author.

Published in 2006 in the U.S. by arrangement with Maureen Moran Agency.

U.K. Hardcover ISBN 1–4056–3570–3 (Chivers Large Print)
U.S. Softcover   ISBN 0–7862–8192–8 (Buckinghams)

The text of this Large Print edition is unabridged.
Other aspects of the book may vary from the original edition.

Set in 16 pt. New Times Roman.

Printed in Great Britain on acid-free paper.

British Library Cataloguing in Publication Data available

Library of Congress Cataloging-in-Publication Data

Converse, Jane.
    Nurse in danger / by Jane Converse.
       p.   cm.
    "Thorndike Press large print Buckinghams"—T.p. verso.
    ISBN 0–7862–8192–8 (lg. print : sc : alk. paper)
    1. Nurses—Fiction. 2. Large type books. I. Title.
PS3553.O544N885 2005
813'.54—dc22   2005023823

Chapter 1

It's all different this morning, Audrey West thought, *though it shouldn't be.*

She had performed as 'scrub nurse' with this same surgical team many times before, and the only change now was that Dr. Voss, who would be retiring next month from a long and distinguished surgical practice, was 'scrubbing in' with Dr. Dan Agnew and the resident assistant, Dr. Reigel. The presence of the elderly cardiac specialist was occasioned by his interest in the young patient and his pride in having contributed to Dan Agnew's knowledge of heart surgery; in no sense was Dr. Voss' last-minute appearance a reason for nervousness. If anything, it gave strength to the team. There was no accounting for her intuitive feeling that something was different . . . something was wrong.

While they scrubbed, the operating surgeon and the older man whose professional suite he shared exchanged what might have passed as lighthearted banter. Audrey had heard them exchange golf scores at times like this; *why* was it different this morning?

'The trick in reassuring a patient's family,' Dr. Voss said, 'is to find a happy medium. In this case, if you tell them a mitral commissurotomy is the . . . let's call it the appendectomy of cardiac surgery, you get them to relax, sure. But you belittle your own value. They get the idea that any schoolboy with a penknife and reasonably steady nerves can handle it. And, Danny, my boy, you suffer the repercussions when you present your bill. On the other hand, if they start conjuring up a layman's picture of dilating a heart valve . . .'

Dr. Voss shook his head, and Dan Agnew interrupted, 'You know this patient's "family." Her mother was killed when she was two. Can you visualize explaining operative techniques to her father? Or can you see Roger Castle arguing about a damned bill when his child's life is at stake?'

'I suppose not, Dan.'

'He's hysterical with fear, and he's going to stay that way no matter what approach we use.' Dan lifted his eyes to the clock on the wall. Audrey recognized the resigned sigh; those hands seemed to stand still whenever you were timing this aseptic procedure. Working antiseptic soap under his nails with the stiff brush, Dan Agnew continued, 'It's like operating with a gun under your ribs. A sort of make-her-well-or-else procedure. At least that was my impression of Mr. Castle. You can't explain mitral stenosis to the man. He isn't interested in how or if. He only knows what.'

'His little girl's a precious child,' Audrey commented. 'I stopped by to see her in her

2

room yesterday.'

There was a stiff silence before the wizened, gray-haired surgeon acknowledged Audrey's reference to their patient. 'Going on six. Not too many years back, she wouldn't have gone much beyond.'

There was no need to detail the child's suffering from a severe attack of rheumatic fever a year before, or the all-too-common aftereffects. Edges of the mitral heart valve had become inflamed. Scarred, thickened, rigid, the valve had lost its elasticity and had narrowed, obstructing the vital flow of blood. And Dr. Voss was recalling a day in the not-too-distant past when Bonnie Castle would have been doomed to a brief life as a semi-invalid. A comparatively simple, yet ingenious operation had been devised to tip the scales in her favor . . . although she would never be restored to a completely normal, active life. But Bonnie Castle would play again. Her life expectancy would be extended, just as a surgeon's finger would separate the adhesions of her damaged heart valve. At least, that was the way it was ninety percent of the time.

And ordinarily, because this gleaming steel-and-tile room was as familiar to her as the living room of the modest duplex apartment she shared with Irene Rafferty, Audrey West would have dismissed the thought of any rising tension within herself or the others. They were at home here, weren't they? Every

3

minute detail of the room's furnishings was as familiar and reassuring to them as they might be strange and frightening to a layman: the I.V. and sponge stands, the prep table, the Mayo stand above the instrument table, the anesthesia and suction machines, the operating table itself under the all-illuminating, shadowless glare of the huge overhead light.

A probationer or a green med student might feel this irrational queasiness, but not the scrub nurse who for more than a year had briskly handed sponges, sutures, and instruments to many surgeons in whom she had confidence, but never the confidence she reserved for the man she loved.

And this was Dr. Dan Agnew, holding out his arms for the sterile gown and rubber gloves; Dan Agnew, in whose strong, sensitive hands a mitral commissurotomy was almost a routine operation. Dr. Voss' joking comparison; what had he said? 'The appendectomy of cardiac surgery.' Everyday procedure!

It persisted—the strange, unfounded sensation that somehow this morning was not the same as all others. Audrey made a quick survey of the operating room, seeking justifications for her suddenly taut nerves. There were none. With Phyllis Leonard in charge of supplies, under the supervision of Mrs. Waldron, a chief O.R. nurse known for her hawkeyed perfection, the stage was

4

flawlessly set. Joanie Hazelrigg was circulating; you could depend on her to supply whatever additional instruments or materials were needed when they were needed and not a quarter of a second later. Dr. Blair . . . if ever an anesthetist had combined science with art . . . and Drs. Agnew, Voss, Reigel . . . no, there was no excuse here for any qualms.

Audrey's close-cropped red hair was hidden under the tightly fitted surgical cap. *It's lack of sleep,* she decided. Lying awake, daydreaming . . . wondering how long a young surgeon had to practice before he permitted himself the luxury of admitting he was in love.

That was it, not enough sleep. Otherwise, there wouldn't be this unprofessional apprehension—what was done each day in this room was not cloaked with fear or mystery if you understood your own place on the team and respected the dedicated skill of the others. This nonsense of imagining furtive, uneasy glances above the green surgical masks! She would be listening for minor, tremolo chords next—the suspense-creating sounds and theatrical gimmicks that movie producers invariably used in crucial operating-room scenes! Pictures were produced within walking distance of Hollywood Memorial Hospital, but the fearful expressions of actor-surgeons were worlds removed from this real-life O.R.

Dan Agnew had taken her to see one of

these medical sagas once, and while they drove home afterward he had laughed. 'So the patient pulled through—fine! But three doctors, four nurses, and an orderly keeled over from hyper-

tension before they got him off the table! The state that leading man was in . . . he couldn't have pulled a thorn out of an airedale's paw, let alone ad-lib a new technique in craniotomy.'

And Dan had been right. Oh, not that some element of suspense didn't always accompany a grave responsibility, or that any doctor or nurse ever took a casual attitude toward a surgical patient. On the contrary, it was *because* they were thoroughly impressed with the importance of their work that they brought calm efficiency into this room, knowing, as no one outside the profession could possibly know, that unless their years of training and experience had developed confidence along with skill, they did not belong. For a hand that hesitated or trembled for one moment here would have reason to tremble again and again . . .

Audrey West reminded herself of that fact as a tiny patient with curly black hair drifted into induced sleep, and again as the plastic endotracheal tube, through which general anesthesia and an unobstructed passage of air would be maintained, was passed into the child's windpipe. Seconds after Dr. Blaire

6

made his customary terse comment, 'You can prep,' signifying that Bonnie Castle was anesthetized and ready for surgery, Dan Agnew's scrub nurse needed no further mental discipline. Not while the operative field was cleansed and painted, not while the patient was draped with sterile towels and sheets, not while Dr. Agnew made his unflinching incision.

There was no time for doubt or concern while the drawstring suture was made about the auricle, the valve dilated, and the sutures drawn taut to prevent loss of blood. During that time, Audrey's attention was concentrated on quick responses to Dan Agnew's crisp commands.

It wasn't until a moment before the incision was sutured that the questioning sensation overcame her again. Ironically, it returned with a brief exchange of worried, knowing glances between the operating surgeon and his more experienced consultant, Dr. Voss; their expressions were so reminiscent of that tension-packed motion-picture scene that Audrey could almost imagine the minor-keyed knife chord in the background.

*   *   *

Bonnie Castle had been wheeled to the recovery room, her postoperative condition good despite her natural frailty. Dr. Reigel, the young resident, accompanied her, and the anesthetist left the room moments afterward.

While Audrey and the circulating R.N., Joan Hazelrigg, restored the O.R. to its previous immaculate condition, Drs. Voss and Dan Agnew lingered near the door.

Dan was obviously concerned; his dark eyes appeared clouded, and his handsome face had taken on a worried appearance not typical of him.

'You'd better get your bearings before you go out to see Castle,' Dr. Voss told him. 'More creases in your forehead than in your gown.'

Normally, Dan would have grinned at the comparison of his face with a sterile, green, unpressed surgical outfit. Now, Audrey watched the frown deepen. 'How could I have missed it?' he asked, more of himself than the other doctor. He rattled off references to a 'sphygmograph,' 'systolometer,' and 'sphygmomanometer' . . . none of what he said completely intelligible to Audrey, but apparently familiar to his colleague in heart surgery.

'You pinpointed mitral stenosis,' Dr. Voss said. 'I examined her, too, remember. And there was *nothing*, Dan! Nothing to indicate a concurrent stenosis of the aortic valve.'

'We could have been set up! With a heart pump . . . we could have taken care of both problems this morning.' Dan closed his eyes momentarily, rubbing the back of his wrist across the bridge of his nose. 'Any ideas, Doctor?'

'Ideas? Oh . . . about explaining to Castle that the child's going to require further surgery.' Dr. Voss sighed. 'Tell him that ausculation at the third intercostal space, close to the left of the sternum, can obscure a murmur behind the third inter—'

'Thanks,' Dan muttered. 'That'll be a great help!' He slapped the older doctor's shoulder playfully, but his annoyance with himself, and the dread of breaking the bad news to an apparently unreasonable parent, were clearly visible.

'If that doesn't do it, tell him another truth.' Dr. Voss pushed open one of the wide O.R. doors, and Dan Agnew followed him out of the room. 'Tell him you went through med school, you didn't descend from Mount Olympus. There's an even bigger shortage of infallible gods than of nurses.'

Dan's dejection remained behind him. Added to the sympathetic misery was Audrey's personal disappointment. There hadn't been a moment to discuss the possibility of meeting downstairs for lunch— no time for him to ask if she were free this evening . . . or tomorrow night . . . or the next. There were no operations scheduled for Dr. Agnew until Monday morning, and unless he made one of his abrupt, unheralded decisions to phone for a date later, the weekend would stretch interminably before her, uneventful and lonely.

Along with her ability as a 'chase nurse,' Joan Hazelrigg had a talent for clairvoyance. '*You're* going to be a cheerful kid to be around until three o'clock,' she said facetiously.

Audrey shrugged her shoulders hopelessly. 'Let's start setting up the eleven-thirty laparotomy, hm?'

'And let's not change the subject, hm?' Joan cleared the instrument tray, walking to the sink as she added, 'Talk about a casual character! How can he date you on and off— make like you're his property one day, and act as though you didn't exist the next?'

'He was upset just now.'

Joan nodded. 'I guess. Gee, that poor little thing . . . having to go through all this again! An even more risky operation, actually. And then not really being all well.' She set the soiled instruments on a stainless steel sink counter. 'I s'pose you're right. Dr. Agnew's blaming himself for not knowing she had an aortic condition, too. He wasn't in any mood for romance.'

Audrey succumbed to an irresistible laugh. '*Romance?* Joanie, you're not serious!'

'Well, I don't expect him to mumble sweet nothings into your ear with a catlin in one hand and a Number Two S needle in the other, no. But if I had your figure and your personality . . . and if I had sexy green eyes . . .'

10

'Oh, come off it, Hazelrigg!'

'I mean it! If I wasn't twenty pounds overweight and I had that crazy red hair instead of this mole fuzz on top of my fat face . . .' Joan tugged at a lock of her prematurely graying hair in a totally unresentful but disparaging gesture.

'You'd what?'

'I'd be married to him by now.'

'Uhuh.'

'I would!'

'For the record, Joanie, he's not ready to be tied down. Too much to learn, too much work ahead of him.'

'One of those superdedicated docs,' Joan said acidly. 'No time in their busy lives for anything but scalpels, sutures, scissors, and saws. I've seen the type. About the time they've got every nurse in the county carrying a torch, they run into some bundle of fluff who only wears flat white shoes to play tennis at some country club. And zam! Young Hippocrates falls on his face.'

Audrey smiled. 'Not Dr. Agnew. Honestly, sometimes I think he doesn't know how to relax. Oh, he'll be . . . sort of fun on a date. But just about the time you think . . .' She stopped, too embarrassed to verbalize the many letdowns.

'Just about the time you think the guy's human, he gets a faraway look in his eye,' Joan said. 'And then he explains why he

11

prefers to use Sim's abdominal tenaculum over Kelly's. I don't get out much, but I recognize the breed. Dedicated. With a big capital D.'

'Dr. Agnew's had it rough.' The rationalization sounded hollow, and Audrey went on to explain, 'He didn't have anybody to finance his training. When you work that hard, you . . . well, it becomes a habit. And then you want to make the most of your chance when you get it.' She didn't have to tell Joan that any of a hundred young surgeons would have given their eyeteeth for an opportunity to work closely with Dr. Voss . . . or to take over that retiring surgeon's practice.

Joan appeared unconvinced. 'Capital Doctor, Capital Daniel, Capital Dedicated Agnew. Take my advice, Audrey. Teach him to relax, even if you have to resort to sedatives.'

'Sure. Be aggressive! Ring wedding bells in his ears!'

'If you don't, somebody else will.' Joan checked her watch. 'You could use a coffee break about now.'

'We'd better lay out the . . .'

'I'll get Phyllis to help me. Look, soon as he's finished talking to the patient's father, he'll want three things, right?'

'Coffee, a cigarette . . .'

'And an understanding female ear,' Joan finished. 'Couldn't you just happen to be in the staffcaf when he comes in?'

'Staffcaf' was hospital jargon for the staff cafeteria. It sounded like a promising suggestion, but Audrey hesitated. 'Mrs. Waldron might not like it if . . .'

'I'll explain the emergency. And bear in mind that Mrs. Waldron's chunkier than I am.'

'Meaning?'

Joan grinned. 'Meaning she's got a big, fat romantic heart. It's a cardiac symptom peculiar to overweight O.R. nurses, sometimes extending to supervisors. Beat it, West.'

Audrey squeezed the plump wrist affectionately. 'You're a honey, Hazelrigg.'

'Just say you caught me in one of my sentimental moments,' Joan said noncommittally. 'Most of the time I'm colder'n surgical steel.'

She managed to maintain the poker-faced pose of indifference until Audrey had reached the door. But, looking back, Audrey decided Miss Hazelrigg, R.N., bore a remarkable resemblance to a slightly overweight cupid in flat white oxfords.

Chapter 2

Audrey's meeting with Dan Agnew came before she expected it.

She took time to shed the unflattering surgical costume and to inspect her crisp white uniform before a mirror in the nurses' lounge.

As always, the warm O.R. temperature had played havoc with even her minimum make-up, and Audrey daubed at it hopefully, attempting to see herself as Dan Agnew would see her.

Short, unlacquered nails, flat shoes, and a shiny face! Fortunately, Dan had a deep respect for the reasons behind her lack of surface glamor. Joanie had been wrong; he wouldn't ever fall on his face over 'some bundle of fluff.' Surgery was his life, and the pinkish, heat-glazed complexion of the hard-working scrub nurse was as acceptable to him as the smell of ether.

Audrey took the elevator down to the main floor and followed a corridor that led past a visitor's vestibule to the staff rooms beyond. Near the inevitable cigarette machine in the waiting room, she saw him. Dr. Agnew (amazing the way she was able to press a mental button that designated when he was Dan and when he was Dr. Agnew) was talking to a man whose thick, curling black hair was almost enough to identify him as Bonnie Castle's father.

Audrey concentrated on reaching her destination; the object was to spend a few moments with Dr. Agnew *alone.* But he spotted her and called out, 'Miss West.' There was no recourse but to join him and the expensively suited, suntanned man whose short, stocky figure was compensated for by a cool look of self-assurance.

Seconds later, Audrey was being introduced to Roger Castle.

'Miss West was virtually my right hand during the operation,' Dr. Agnew was saying.

Apparently he had explained the necessity for further surgery on Bonnie to the man's satisfaction, because Mr. Castle acknowledged the introduction with a powerful handshake, meanwhile inspecting Audrey with a critical, expert eye. He owned a talent agency and a number of nightclubs and gambling casinos, Audrey had heard. The embarrassing sweep of those black, unsmiling eyes was probably a professional habit; he couldn't help the appraising stare.

And the sharp impression given by his attire was dispelled by a raspy, guttural voice and coarse, wrong-side-of-the-tracks diction. 'Nice meetin' you, honey. You gave Doc here a big hand, so you'll get taken care of. I don't ferget, see?'

'I've been trying to tell Mr. Castle that we do our best for *every* patient,' Dan said. 'If Bonnie had been a charity case, we . . .'

'O.K., O.K.' Roger Castle held up a plumpish, hairy, but immaculately manicured hand; an ostentatious ring glittered as he gestured. 'O.K., you got what it takes, you pass it aroun'. I'll buy that. What I'm tellin' you, when you save *my* kid's life, that's where *I* say what goes. An' I say I wanna fix up anybody had anything t' do with pullin' Bonnie through.'

His crude evaluation of how the medical profession functioned shocked Audrey. And it was obviously embarrassing to Dr. Agnew. 'Mr. Castle, we . . .'

Apparently Castle could be as affable as he was obnoxious, switching from one phase to the next easily. 'All right. All right, you told me about another operation. That's better than I heard before, an' I hired the best. I got a sick little kid there—think I don't know? So what it takes to make her O.K., you do it. An' I mean, you do *everything*. I got no use fer half the people I know, you follow me? I could live without most of the other fifty percent. But this kid . . .' Roger Castle's eyes narrowed, but an alien softness had crept in to blot out the steely, suspicious chill. 'This kid . . . what I mean—I don't give a damn about nobody else like I . . .' His face colored, adding a ruddy glow to a tan that had obviously been cultivated under costly health-club lamps in a successful effort to combat the sickly pallor of the night time operator. Husky, his voice betrayed what his crude articulation failed to get across. 'Bonnie needs somethin', it's gonna be there. Know what I mean?'

Dr. Agnew nodded. It didn't take a psychologist to know that in a vast empire of cynicism and power, Roger Castle had one refuge, one island where his need for human love was met. He'd destroy anyone who stood in his way, Audrey decided. But the man's love for his motherless child was genuine, fanatically genuine. It was a shuddering thought to consider how he would have reacted if Bonnie hadn't pulled through that commissurotomy with a strengthened heart. 'You say she needs another operation,' he said thickly. 'It's gonna be the best. I want *you*. Follow me, Doc? The best!'

In Castle's uncomplicated black-and-white world, a world in which there were only those who were for him, or against him, deserving of corresponding reward or retribution, Dr. Agnew and his nurse had won the Napoleonic blessing. It wasn't the man's fault that he could offer no more imaginative a thank you than an offer of money. Crudely, ostentatiously, he assured Dr. Agnew that he would be 'taken care of.'

Uneasily, Dan suggested that a more ethical approach would be to lend a financial assist to the hospital. 'We've been in need of an expanded pathology lab,' he said. 'It would benefit a good many patients if we could add equipment and personnel to . . .'

'What'll it take? Thirty grand? Fifty? That do it? Fifty grand? You tell me how you want the check made out, you got it.' Roger Castle appeared immensely satisfied with the stunned reactions, responding to them with a lop-sided, humorless smile. He seemed totally unaware of his coarseness, or of the fact that others might be regarding him as a somewhat pitiable social aborigine.

Probably embarrassed for him, Dan Agnew said, 'That's very kind of you, Mr. Castle.'

'My pals call me Roger.'

'Very considerate of you, Roger.'

'Forget it.' The show-business and gambling kingpin waved a hand deprecatingly. 'I'll have my bookkeeper call you. What I wanna know now is, when do I see the kid?'

He accepted without question the doctor's advice that Bonnie not be disturbed until the next day. With her post-operative condition complicated by aortic stenosis, her recovery would be more difficult than Roger Castle surmised; Dan Agnew emphasized that the danger hadn't ended because the child had survived surgery. 'Let's give her as much rest as possible,' he finished.

'You say the word, Doc,' Roger Castle agreed. 'You say wait till tomorrow, I'll buy that. The kid's O.K. now? You're not givin' me the business?'

'She's doing very well under the circumstances.'

Castle shot out his hand, pumping the doctor's in a firm handshake. 'The greatest,' he said. 'You got it made with me, Agnew.' He repeated the brief half-smile for Audrey's benefit. 'You ever want somethin', honey, you know who t' call.'

'Thank you,' Audrey said.

'I'll be in touch, Doc. Don't hold nothin' back . . . the kid gets the best.'

A few seconds later they watched the dapper figure stride toward the glass exit doors, barely gesturing to two burly men who had apparently been waiting for him. They were both outfitted in extreme-cut, tasteless, and rather flashy clothes, in the Hollywood hood tradition. Expressionless, reflecting nothing more than a cold, reptilian wariness, the obvious hirelings accompanied Roger Castle out of the hospital.

'Shades of the bootlegging era,' Dan commented. 'If you were doing a gangster picture and needed a couple of bodyguard types, wouldn't you call Hollywood casting for those two?'

'They looked like the real article to me,' Audrey commented.

'Bodyguards? Oh, come on! This guy's a legitimate operator.'

'Uhuh.' Audrey smiled. 'One of the boys came along for the ride because it's such a lovely day. And the other's a minister. That bulge over his hips was undoubtedly a Bible.'

'Audrey, the man's a respectable businessman. A multi-millionaire, from what I've heard. A little rough around the edges, maybe . . . He probably made it the hard way. But he's . . . gad, anyone who can contribute fifty thousand dollars to a hospital without giving it two seconds' thought . . .'

'. . . is somebody who makes it the easy way,' Audrey insisted.

Dan shrugged his shoulders. 'You know what they say around town: that's show biz. Were you going for coffee?'

'Yes.'

Imitating Roger Castle's back-alley delivery, Dan said expansively, 'You wanna cuppa coffee, honey, money's no object. It's on me.'

He seemed to have shaken off the earlier depression, and Audrey felt relieved.

On their way to the staff cafeteria, he shook his head in amazement. 'Wait'll I tell the administrators they can junk some of that antiquated equipment in Pathology.'

'Mr. Castle was quite impressed with you,' Audrey said.

Walking beside Audrey, Dan told her, 'He hasn't the faintest comprehension of what's involved. Seems to have an idea that you can buy medical results the way you buy Cadillacs.' He shook his head, still bewildered by the recent conversation. 'You know, he accepted the need for a second operation without asking *one question!*'

'You brought his little girl through surgery.'

'Exactly. And on that basis he's decided I can do no wrong.'

'My impression was that he thinks this way,' Audrey said. 'If you succeed for him, you're a

20

hero. If you . . .'

She stopped abruptly, not wanting to grind into Dan Agnew's consciousness the possibility that his patient might *not* recover. And there was a second crisis to be faced, perhaps within two or three months. No one could predict the results. The only certainty was that Roger Castle's stark friend-or-foe mind would react as sharply to failure as it had to success.

Dan should have interpreted her silence. Surely he was sensitive enough to know that Castle's overwhelming approval of him might be reversed, perhaps violently, through circumstances beyond surgical control. But evidently his relief at not being questioned about the incomplete diagnosis, and his exuberance over Castle's generous contribution, blotted out any future problems. 'Quite a guy,' he said. 'One of those diamonds in the rough you hear about.'

'He's a diamond, all right,' Audrey admitted.

They had come to the cafeteria door, and Dan stopped to explore her face quizzically. 'Were you being facetious? Or do you mean he has a sparkling personality?'

'No, I was . . . thinking in terms of . . . value,' Audrey explained.

'Oh. Yes, I guess he's worth plenty.'

She didn't mention her intuitive feeling about Roger Castle, or the other function of diamonds. In industry, weren't they known for their quality of hardness? Known to cut or drill through anything placed in their way?

Before the coffee break ended, Joan Hazelrigg's romantic engineering produced the desired result. Dan ended the session with an unheralded, matter-of-fact reference to the effect that he had nothing doing Saturday night, and if Audrey had no plans, why didn't they stir up something? This casual approach was always somewhat disheartening; there was the suspicion that if she had said she was busy, he would have nodded and changed the subject without any further ado. Still, when you loved a man, a careless invitation was better than none at all . . .

*   *   *

It was close to the Appointed Hour of Eight, Saturday evening, and Audrey had been dressed for her date with Dan Agnew since six. Dressed, undressed, redressed, undressed, and dressed again, because somewhere along the line she had decided that the white wool with its low-scooped neckline was too showy and would give Dan the impression that she considered this a big night in her life. Over the head with it, mussing her hair so that it looked not merely nonchalant, but impossibly careless.

'Like a nest of red feathers,' Irene Rafferty

had observed flatly.

Then the pine green suit hadn't looked dressy enough, and she had gone through the whole routine again, with the white wool getting a final nod of approval, followed by repeated hair combing, lipstick retouching, and earring selecting.

'You're going to a Presidential reception? With Cary Grant?' Irene scowled at every change. 'Press photographers waiting?'

Irene's rare smiles were twitchy little movements that stretched her thin lips like snapped rubberbands across her pinched, pink, freckled face. A dietitian at Hollywood Memorial, she looked as though she had been on a weight-reducing kick since the Year One. Uncharitable persons would have called her a dour, rangy scarecrow. If they were terribly fond of Irene, as Audrey was, they might be more inclined to label her tall and slim and a bit on the serious side, though the latter impression would go out the window when some of Irene's screwball enterprises came to light.

Tonight, as was customary around the attractive, furnished duplex she shared with Audrey, the dietitian had hidden her flat figure under a billowing muu-muu—a brilliant green-and-blue print affair that made one think of a mammoth billboard advertising pineapple draped over a tent pole. Irene's long, sand-colored hair was wrapped in tight coils above her narrow face, a top-heavy effect that she somehow counterbalanced by wearing loose-fitting Mexican huaraches on her elongated feet. Irene was a firm believer in natural comfort, unhampered by the 'circulation-stopping restrictions imposed by fashion.' This ungainly ensemble was not enhanced by the inevitable smudges of mimeograph ink on her forehead and arms.

Inspecting Audrey as though dressing up for a date was the height of the ludicrous, Irene continued her caustic interview. 'Kind of a tight dress to wear while bowing before the queen, wouldn't you say?'

Audrey frowned. 'Irene, you'll have me feeling overdressed again. I want to look nice, but if you think . . .'

'Ye Gods, she's going to start the strip-tease act again!' Irene pressed a bony hand against her forehead. 'Oh, no! Not another switch! You look fine, Audrey. Please . . . I'm not up to facing any more major decisions. It's not that important!'

'It is to me.'

Irene was adamant. 'If a man likes you, he'll accept you the way you are.'

'Irene . . . Dr. Agnew isn't Charley Perkins!'

'Meaning his values are all misplaced? Meaning he . . . judges human beings by superficial, external . . .'

'Irene, honey, *not* another lecture! I'm all on edge as it is!'

24

Irene plunked herself down on the living-room rug, sitting in what Audrey presumed was one of the yoga positions most beneficial to the respiratory system. Sitting cross-legged, with the unnecessary yards of blue-green-pineapple fabric surrounding her like a collapsed parachute, Irene said, 'Exactly. Exactly my point. You're all strung up. Now, if you and Dr. Agnew shared one genuine interest in common . . .'

'But we work together! I'm in surgery with him almost every . . .'

'. . . one truly spontaneous interest in common,' Irene went on stubbornly, 'you wouldn't feel obligated to put on a big show for his benefit. And you wouldn't be in this inharmonious, health-destroying state. Proves he's all wrong for you. Furthermore, if . . .'

'If I lived on dried figs, yogurt, and . . . all those goofy grains and unrecognizable things out in the kitchen . . . all that hay . . .'

'You'd have your nervous system responding accordingly,' Irene announced.

How Irene managed to reconcile her faddist notions about nutrition with the varied diets prescribed at the hospital Audrey didn't even dare to guess. The point was that when she traded her white uniform for the at-home muu-muu, Irene practiced and preached her way-out health food doctrine as The Law; any problem, from aching feet to trouble in figuring out your income tax, was directly

25

attributable to a faulty, un-Rafferty diet.

Audrey made a last-minute inspection of her seams. 'Well, you wanted me to have something in common with Dan Agnew. There it is.'

Irene scowled. 'There *what is*?'

'We both like steaks.'

Audrey laughed, and the often-repeated argument ended with Irene's grudging admission: 'That's a fair start. Providing . . .'

'I know. Providing we eat them raw. Trouble is, we'll probably go to Perino's for dinner, not the Griffith Park Zoo.'

The door chimes sounded, and Audrey made a nervous start toward the foyer.

'That could be Charley,' Irene said flatly. 'We're going to run off circulars about our booklet . . . you know, the new one, *Add Ten Years to Your Life with Unbleached Flour*. Did I tell you we bought this terrific new mailing list . . . recent raw honey customers? We should sell thousands of copies.'

Audrey had heard the same hopeful beginnings of a dozen other grandiose health food mail-order schemes hatched by Irene and her colorless little beau, Big-Idea Charley, who invariably came up with a zany new plan on the very day his previous brainstorm died an ignominious death. They made a compatible threesome—Irene, Charley and their duplicating machine (the latter an inky monster that monopolized the apartment's dining area). For Audrey, at least at the moment, their next venture held absolutely no interest.

She opened the door and, in the next second, had to fight back the revealing breathlessness that always accompanied Dan's entrance into a room. Somehow he looked less casual than usual; certainly he had made an extra effort to present a fashionable picture, and there was an eagerness in his expression that implied this might be an important evening for him, too.

Most amazingly, he seemed pleased with Audrey's appearance, opening their conversation with the most complimentary phrase she had ever heard from him, 'Talk about Women in White!' followed by a quick, low, highly unprofessional whistle.

Audrey felt herself coloring as Dan surveyed the close fit of the white wool sheath. Until now he had seemed almost indifferent. 'It's not . . . too much?'

Dan laughed, following her into the room. 'That's the word for it, nursie. Too much!' He stopped to exchange clipped hellos with Irene, who had spotted a book within reaching distance of her position on the floor and was absorbed in its contents, then returned his attention to Audrey, grinning broadly. 'Really too much!'

Confused, Audrey was considering a change back to the green suit when Dan plucked her brocade jacket from a chair back and began helping her into it. 'Where we're going, you'd probably feel comfortable in a sequined formal.'

'Oh? Where's that?'

'I know one thing,' Irene muttered. 'It's someplace where they cook all the vitamins out of your dinner.'

Audrey shot her a pleading glance, and Dan explained, 'We have an after-dinner invitation. A party. In Beverly Hills.'

'Well, now I am impressed!' (Irene and that acid tone! Why did she have to be so critical . . . make Dan feel unwelcome?)

'Doctor who?' Audrey asked. Any number of the attending physicians Dan knew at the hospital lived in Beverly Hills.

'Doctor nobody. Look, I'm starved. I'll tell you all about it on the way.' Dan was guiding her toward the door. 'We got an invitation from Roger Castle.'

'He's giving a party . . . with his little girl just out of surgery and . . .'

'A celebration,' he said. 'Movie stars, wheels, V.I.P.'s. "A real bash," is the way he put it.'

'Dan, that's unheard of!'

'I tried to tell him that, but . . . it seems there's one perpetual party at his house. He likes having people around.'

'He'd better get used to having it quiet when Bonnie comes home,' Audrey said.

'Oh, he's planning to shift the scene of action to his place in Palm Springs when she's released from the hospital. Three Specials to look after her . . . God knows, she won't be neglected.'

'But a party? Tonight?' Audrey shook her head in disbelief.

'It takes all kinds,' Irene commented from behind her book. 'The world is full of oddballs.'

Dan turned, and his eyes swept over the wild-colored muu-muu, the enormous thong sandals that protruded from under that nest of yardage, and finally Irene's seriocomic face. 'Yes, isn't it?' he agreed politely. 'Kooky characters everywhere you look.'

Irene let the remark pass, replying with a solemn nod. 'I hear some of them eat boiled vegetables and cooked meat. How kooky can you get?'

Having traded discreet insults, the pair seemed satisfied that there was no more to say; Dan shrugged his shoulders, and Irene returned to her reading.

Outside, the April evening promised to be cool and fresh, but the anticipated hours with Dan had suddenly been dampened by Roger Castle's invitation. Dan hadn't 'dressed up' for this date; his enthusiasm and unexpected attention to Audrey's appearance were probably related to the party. He wasn't looking forward to being alone with her; Dan

Agnew apparently preferred the company of a glamorous crowd!

Audrey's disappointment was intensified as Dan helped her into his car. 'Should be interesting,' he said, 'seeing how the other half lives. At least we won't be doing the same old thing.'

The same old thing! Talking, having a quiet dinner together, sometimes holding hands during a play or a movie, on rare occasions kissing each other good night. Nothing exciting, nothing hopeful, but when had it ever been dull? Not to me, Audrey thought. But for Dan, 'the same old thing' was obviously not enough!

During dinner, at a candle-lighted table for two, Dan admitted that Roger Castle's invitation intrigued him.

'Castle gave me quite a pitch. I told him I'm not much for parties, and he claimed working too hard can ruin a man. Maybe he's right.'

'I hate to say "I told you so," ' Audrey said.

'All right, I need a little relaxation. I haven't begun to enjoy California. You'd think I was still holed up in a cell, serving my residency in Chicago. This is a great place for living it up, but I haven't done it.'

'I've been trying to tell you that for a year, Dan.'

'Then I think that taking over Dr. Voss' practice is an immense responsibility . . . a tremendous challenge.'

'But you can't stop living, Dan!'

Dan concentrated on his steak for a moment, then responded with a disheartening reply. 'That's right. You can't stop living, Audrey. You've got to enjoy life as opportunities to enjoy it arise. What an up-and-coming surgeon has to guard against isn't *fun*—that's where I've made my mistake—but he has to make certain he doesn't take on additional responsibilities.'

'I don't understand. You haven't ever talked about taking on new responsibilities—aside from your practice, I mean.'

A corner of Dan's mouth twisted upward in an ironic, almost sheepish grin. 'Let's say I've given it some thought.'

'Thought about? . . .'

'Getting married,' Dan said simply.

He didn't elaborate, and the embarrassed silence that followed indicated that the now-discarded thought had revolved around Audrey. Time and again he had revealed that he dated no one else; evenings he spent without her were spent in study, in long after-dinner conversations at the Voss residence, or in informal bull sessions with colleagues whose operative techniques interested him. Nor was there a remembered childhood sweetheart from the past; Dan had burned all of his romantic bridges behind him, if, indeed, any serious liaisons had ever existed.

A mingled exultation and disillusionment

stirred inside Audrey; hope unexpectedly kindled and as abruptly snuffed into ashes. With a man who hadn't considered marrying her, there was always the encouraging possibility that he might. But Dan Agnew had apparently measured the pros and cons of a marriage with Audrey West and discarded the idea.

'I wish you hadn't told me that,' Audrey said quietly.

Dan explained that he enjoyed her company over anyone else's because he could be completely honest with her. 'I . . . I didn't think I'd have to weigh every word I said to you. We're good friends,' he continued lamely. 'I wouldn't be this frank with someone I didn't care for, would I?' He seemed to realize that the hollow platitude would have been better left unsaid.

Dinner continued awkwardly, Dan changing from one subject to another in abortive attempts to restore the usual relaxed atmosphere. With resentment adding itself to the conflicting emotions churning inside Audrey, the banal comments died of neglect. They left the restaurant separated by a wordless tension, Audrey dreading the prospect of putting on a gay façade for the benefit of strangers, and Dan undoubtedly wishing he hadn't delved into the topic of 'added responsibility.'

In the semidarkness of the restaurant's

parking lot, Dan's hand tightened on her forearm as he helped her into his car. It may have been a warm, reassuring gesture, or it may have been an outward display of pity. Audrey swallowed hard, turning toward Dan in the next moment. 'Please don't,' she said.

'Don't? . . .'

'Don't be patronizing or sympathetic . . . or . . .' Audrey caught her breath, seeking control of her voice. 'What I'm trying to say is . . . this may be Hollywood, but I'm a stranger here when it comes to that "we can still be friends" routine.' Dan tried to object, but she stopped him. 'And, Dan, please spare me a surprised reaction. If you say, "but I didn't know you cared!" I'll either take a cab home or I'll splash salt water all over your pretty front-seat upholstery.'

He stood there for a moment next to the opened car door, his grip tightening on her arm, his eyes examining her face in the faint light. 'You'll have a devil of a time finding a cab,' he said finally. 'So cry on the upholstery, honey, because I'm going to say it.' Dan's voice dropped to a husky, resonant depth, his affection for her unmistakable now. 'I didn't know you cared.'

Audrey heard herself sniff, an unladylike sound that threatened to unnerve her completely. Then she was sitting next to the driver's seat, composing herself, waiting for Dan to half-circle the car and join her, and thinking it was ridiculous to be recalling a corny scrap of verse from Kipling: 'And I would have, now that love is o'er, An end to all, an end; I cannot, having been your lover, stoop to become your friend.'

Ridiculous to recall those sentimental and inappropriate lines, because Dan had never been any more than a friend—a friend who kissed her good night occasionally . . .

Dan got into the car, barely slamming the door behind him before he pulled her into his arms. The assertive move left her no time to think or to protest. He made one brief, gruffly spoken remark: 'And just in case you think I'm feeling sorry for you, you're wrong!'

Whatever reply she might have made was buried under the intensity of his mouth pressed against hers and the possessive clasp of her body against his. And if he didn't love her, Audrey thought ecstatically, he was wasting his life in medicine; he was the world's most gifted actor!

When Dan released her, both of them breathing hard, Audrey waited for an admission that he had been mistaken; that a woman he loved would not be a detriment but an asset to his medical career . . . waited for him to remember that she was a surgical nurse who had worked beside him, appreciated the demands of his profession, would understand the sacrifices entailed in furthering his development as a surgeon.

If he was thinking along these lines, Dan Agnew was too shaken to tell her so. Audrey heard him start up the motor, heard his chagrined attempt at joking dismissal: 'Fine thing. Necking in a parking lot, like high school kids.'

Audrey forced herself to join the facetious mood. 'I think the current term is "making out."'

Dan laughed, a thin, nervous laugh. And it wasn't until he was steering the car through the congested Saturday night traffic of Sunset Boulevard that his tone grew more somber and he said, 'Give me time, Audrey. If I hadn't given up so much . . . just for the right to practice surgery . . .' He shook his head, suddenly inarticulate.

'I know. If you were a soda jerk, you wouldn't have to think twice about saddling yourself with a wife and . . .'

'Maybe a family,' Dan finished. He was deadly serious now. 'Oh, I know what I'd like, but also know what I've got to do. I'm not sure that the two are compatible. At least not . . . just yet.' He turned to smile at Audrey—again that self-conscious, uncertain grin that revealed his inner confusion. And he was aware of that confusion, apologizing for it in the next breath. 'Call me a crazy, mixed-up kid? I need a little time for thought . . . and I'd hate to think I might lose you during that process.'

'You won't lose me,' Audrey admitted. The phrase sounded stilted and somewhat weak to her ears. Tomorrow she might regret having told Dan that she loved him . . . that she would be waiting when and if he was ready to have her. Now . . . now it seemed the only alternative; a poor and somewhat humiliating compromise.

'I've been driving myself so long . . . so long, with no time to . . .'

'Don't explain,' she told him. 'When you're sure of yourself, tell me. Right now, I'd rather drop it.'

'Still want to go home? You wanted to, didn't you?'

Audrey nodded.

'If you want to skip this thing at Castle's . . .'

'Skipping it' would have meant an end to the evening, an end to being with Dan. It would have meant going to an apartment now occupied by two people whose solidarity would only underscore her loneliness; and wasn't an undecided Dan Agnew better than a Dan Agnew who left her alone, possibly to go to Roger Castle's party on his own?

'I'm looking forward to it,' Audrey lied. And forcing a light, devil-may-care tone, she said, 'Who knows? It might be interesting.'

Dan seemed pleased with her decision. 'Might be at that,' he said.

If it troubled her that Dan drove toward Beverly Hills eagerly, chatting about nonessential matters as though nothing had transpired between them, Audrey made no comment. Dissatisfied, disappointed, disillusioned . . . what difference did it make, when just *being* with Dan was so tremendously important?—when a crumb was preferable to no cake at all?

Chapter 3

Roger Castle's home was an isolated island within a city. Though the wrought-iron gates were open, admitting Dan's Oldsmobile into the spacious, parklike grounds, there was an air of protected seclusion about the enormous residence. It was a mammoth, Spanish-style concoction of thick white masonry, red overlapping roof tiles, and arched windows, most of them barred by metal grillwork which lent itself to comparison with the bars of prisons and fortresses.

Hidden spotlights illuminated the property. A flood of near-daylight brightness fell over the row of Brazilian palms bordering the white, crushed-rock driveway that swept toward the massive structure. Less glaring were the blue lights playing over an elaborate fountain, complete with sculptured cupids and the inevitable chubby little Neopolitan urchin pouring water from the inevitable marble urn.

If there were any doubts in Audrey's mind that Castle's castle had been built in the mid-twenties by an affluent and tasteless movie star, they were dispelled when she stepped into the ballroom-sized foyer. The decor, leaning heavily on rococo moldings, ornate tapestries, and massive furniture (gilded and sagging under red velvet upholstery), combined a blending of styles; Mediterranean, Moorish, and *nouveau riche* hoodlum. To verify the latter, a sullen, broad-shouldered butler, who would have looked more at home in a pool hall than a drawing room, established Dan Agnew's identity with an amazingly unbutlerish request to see the doctor's 'credentials.' Dan flashed his wallet. Apparently his driver's license served as an *open sesame*; he and Audrey were escorted toward wide, imposing double doors made up of elaborately carved, dark wooden panels. The doors were opened, revealing a glittering gathering, perhaps thirty people in all. The formally attired muscle boy who had led them into this smoke-hazed, conversation-buzzing room retreated, his heavy-lidded, cobralike expression implying there was something suspect about the new arrivals, Dan's identification papers notwithstanding.

Far across the room, Roger Castle spotted their entrance. Audrey saw him break away from a group that had surrounded him near the bar, then cross the room with a self-assured stride that would have told a complete stranger: 'Roger Castle owns this house . . . owns everything in this room . . . every*one* in this room.'

But his greeting was affable and sincere. 'Glad you kids could make it! No kiddin' . . . this is great!' He shook Dan's hand and complimented Audrey with the same swift, arrogant, head-to-toe sweep of eyes that had embarrassed her at the hospital. 'That's all right!' he muttered—as though he were approving a piece of merchandise, Audrey thought resentfully. For Dan's sake, she managed to smile.

'What's a matter . . . we got no service around here?' Roger snapped his fingers at a white-coated waiter who passed by carrying a tray of hors d'oeuvres. 'Let's get on the ball, uh? I invite friends, I don't want 'em standin' around till you get good an' ready they should have a drink!'

Chagrined, the waiter croaked, 'Sorry, Mr. Castle. I'll get their orders.'

Dan jumped to the old man's rescue: 'No rush. We just this minute walked in, Roger.' The waiter gave Dan an appreciative glance, drinks were ordered, and Roger, satisfied that he had established himself as the conscientious host, led them to the group of people he had been entertaining at the bar.

Famous names, familiar faces! Roger's introductions sounded like he was reading a theatrical *Who's Who* interspersed with obscure names that accompanied less glamorous, cruder faces. Between greetings, Audrey glanced to see Dan's reactions. He was quite obviously impressed, quite obviously enjoying the attention he received from some of the top personalities in show business. Roger made it a point to dramatize the surgeon's operation on his daughter. 'Listen . . . this guy's a genius. Know what I mean? Everybody told me the kid didn't have a chance. Today I walk in her room . . . bring her all these presents, see . . . and she's got a smile for the ole man.'

She's alive, Audrey thought. But with the aortic valve narrowed, Bonnie Castle's far from out of danger. How could Dan stand there and listen to these uninformed, risk-filled praises? Dan might be a 'genius' in Roger's book today, but tomorrow he might be condemned with an equally exaggerated term—he might be a murderer!

Dan must have known this, yet he seemed to be drinking in the adulation of Roger's friends. The most outspoken of these admirers was Ginger Lampton. Her comments, Audrey noticed, combined applause for Dr. Agnew along with an almost obsequious reverence for Roger Castle: 'If Rog' says you're a terrific doctor, that's good enough for me, honey. Rog' doesn't settle for the mediocre. He goes the quality route all the way, you know?'

Roger puffed on his cigar and ignored her; flattery from his 'regular crowd' was probably tiresome to him, even if it was demanded. But Dan smiled appreciatively. Any man just meeting Ginger Lampton would have, Audrey decided glumly.

Ginger was no statuesque beauty. She was short, possibly inclined to plumpness, but the compact figure she had compressed into a low-cut black cocktail dress had been admirably controlled. The effect was one of sensual ripeness, topped by a face that somehow combined mature sophistication with wide, baby-blue-eyed innocence. Her honey-colored hair was smartly coiffed in a rather extreme, shaggy style; heavy make-up, expertly applied, managed to make her look more glamorous than coarse. And, of course, if all other charms had failed, Ginger Lampton could have relied upon the breathy, low, seductive voice that had brought her fame as a night-club chanteuse . . . a voice that had catapulted her in the past year into a number of significant appearances on TV and a contract with a major Hollywood studio.

Suddenly the white wool sheath that had seemed too dressy earlier in the evening felt drab and common. As Ginger directed all of her comments and a not-too-subtle interest toward Dan, Audrey sank into a hopeless, defeated mood. She felt a jealous resentment, too, of the naïve way Dan was gulping down Ginger's studied, ego-building compliments. Couldn't he see through the obvious play for him? Or, worse, was he aware of it, and were his gracious replies meant to encourage the attention?

Roger tired of the conversation. He drifted off toward an adjoining room, a luscious little sloe-eyed brunette linking her arm with his as he made his exit. A few of the movie personalities in the group, as if instinctively conscious that extra company was cramping Ginger's style, broke off and joined other small cliques. The group became a quartet, another man hovering on the sidelines, with only Ginger and Dan present, if one were to judge by the animated conversation.

Then, with a second cocktail, half-consumed, in her hand, Audrey was being steered away from the bar, and someone was saying to her, 'Two's company, four's a mob. Ginny's in high gear tonight, isn't she?'

Audrey looked up to see a face that had beamed out at her in any number of romantic films. And the voice! He wasn't singing now, but she had heard the man's voice on dozens of records. That frank, only faintly dissipated, world-weary face . . . the penetrating hazel eyes. Who? . . .

He edged Audrey to a Victorian sofa secluded from view by a gargantuan stone planter filled with tropical growth. They sat

42

down, and he fixed her with an amused but not unfriendly stare. 'I said, Miss Lampton's turned on all four motors tonight.'

'I wouldn't know,' Audrey mumbled. 'I've . . . never met her before.'

Whoever he was, he lifted his glass and took several deep swallows before he spoke again. When he did, the words came out lazily and without effort—a lulling, crooning effect that stirred in her memory. 'Welcome to the jungle, O red-haired stranger. Now you've met the Big Tiger—that's Roger. You've met the lady panther—that's Ginger. And the big, bad wolf. That's me.'

'I'm not worried about you,' Audrey said honestly.

'Uhuh. Too depressed to be vulnerable. I had you figured.' He waved his glass unsteadily for emphasis. 'Pretty young starlet sees professional man fall into clutches of rising songstress. I had it figured. I'm a swingin' analyst in my spare time, doll. Am I right?'

'All except the "young starlet" part,' Audrey told him. 'I'm not.'

'You're not an old starlet.'

'I'm a nurse.'

He laughed, but he apparently wasn't the type to be surprised at anything. 'Real live nurse, huh? That's a new breed around here.'

'I can prove it,' Audrey said. She held out her hands. 'See? Short fingernails. I work in

43

surgery.' She wasn't in the mood for idle banter, but with this relaxed stranger, she was at least spared the humiliation of being an unwelcome third party at the bar.

He scowled. 'Sounds gruesome.' Then he patted one of her hands between his. 'I repeat: welcome to the jungle, nurse. Come to think of it, your training may be useful in this milieu.' He sighed, grinned crookedly, then sighed again; if she had known him better, Audrey would have told him that he'd had enough to drink. But there was something that reflected her own misery in his voice, in spite of the cynical, smart-aleck tone of his conversation, and she decided he was likable. Whoever he was.

Audrey encouraged him to go on. 'Why would my training be useful?'

'Oh . . . this is Successville, doll. Much kicking, gouging, scratching, and bleeding. It happens during a game called "Getting to the Top." But you know something, Red? If you get up there the easy way, it can be even more painful.'

'What's the easy way?' Audrey asked.

An expression of deep bitterness clouded the handsome, exasperatingly familiar face. 'The easy way, cherub, is being Roger Castle's property.'

'I don't follow you.'

'No, you wouldn't. You're a nurse. But say you're idiotic enough to be an ambitious showgirl. An actress. Or a pop singer. He buys you. Fat, fat percentage. He dresses you, gets you trained, publicizes you . . . shoves you right into the public's face. You see?'

'You'd still have to . . . have talent.'

'That's only ten percent of the game, sweetheart. The ten percent you get to keep. The rest he owns. And you can hate his guts, hate the other things you know about him . . . the really vicious things . . . but you're weak, you see? You like your SL-300 Mercedes and your Olympic-size pool and people asking you for autographs. Hate yourself for being a lousy puppet on strings, sure. Sure, but you can't break away. That's what's known as sure-fire success. Castle-style.'

'I'm ashamed to admit this,' Audrey said. 'But I didn't get your name . . . and, honestly, I don't . . .'

She stopped because he was staring at her with something like wonder. Strangely, he seemed to be pleased with what she had said.

'You're not giving me the business? You really don't know who I am?'

Audrey felt herself blushing. 'I should, I suppose. You're . . . well, I know I've seen your face and heard your voice. But I don't get out too often and . . .'

'And I look better on the screen,' he admitted. 'They jazz you up with make-up . . . you know the bit. But tell me this isn't the craziest! You're sitting here letting me cry on your shoulder. And it's not because you're impressed or star-struck or . . . ambitious? Just to be nice? No kidding?'

He looked so delighted that Audrey forgot her own disappointment and laughed. 'Never heard of you.'

'Well, baby, if this isn't the greatest day in my life! You dig *me*. And you never heard of Jeff Beaumont!'

Audrey caught her breath. No one who read a newspaper, listened to radio or television, watched a wide screen, or listened to records could have missed knowing about him. Jeff Beaumont's name was a household word, and fans who didn't worship his singing voice were addicted to him as an actor. 'I guess you . . . think I'm pretty stupid.'

'No, just pretty. You're a refreshing change. For instance, you're neither going to rip off my necktie for a souvenir, or ask me to introduce you to the right people.'

'No.'

'Cross your heart? No big yen to see your name in lights?'

'Cross my heart.'

He started to laugh again, looking younger and more like the screen idol she should have recognized. Then, abruptly, Jeff's mood sobered, and he said, 'You're in love with the doc?'

Audrey decided he rated an honest answer. 'Yes.'

Jeff shook his head dolefully. 'There's a guy that's star-struck. Impressed big. Ginger's making a thing of it. What makes him so impressionable?'

'He's had a rough life,' Audrey said. 'Not enough fun.'

'Uhhuh. Well, fun's her speciality. By the way, she's one of Roger's legitimate properties. Roger owns lots of people.'

'Is she his? . . .'

'Girl friend? Yeah. Past tense,' Jeff explained. 'Roger gets bored quickly. But she's still on good terms with him. Ginny's a profitable investment. And if she's learned what I know about him—about where his real money comes from, she has sense enough to keep her mouth shut.'

'What have you learned?' Audrey wanted to know.

Jeff eyed her solemnly, and he was quiet for a long time. Then he said, 'Let's just say I have sense enough to keep my mouth shut, too. O.K.? Otherwise you'd know more than it's healthy to know. And that'd be a shame, Red. Because I like you. I can't ask you out, because Roger's publicity boys pick my dates for me . . . and remember I told you, I'm too weak to buck the system. But I'm not going to tell you something it's not smart to know. And I'm not going to make a pass at you, either. Uh-uh. Even though you're one of the rare real people from a world I left behind.' Jeff

47

leaned over to plant a brotherly kiss on Audrey's forehead. 'Not because I don't like you, Red. Strictly because I do.'

They sat in silence for a few moments, sharing the rapport of separate miseries. After a while, Jeff Beaumont said, 'Don't worry about Ginger. She's a headhunter. She's never had a surgeon in her collection, but once she's hung his scalp on her belt, he'll be released.'

'That's a comforting thought,' Audrey said dryly.

'Take it for what it's worth.'

'Thank you.'

'If you ever need a . . . celebrity, for purposes of invoking jealousy in the doc'— Jeff shrugged—'feel free to use my name. But I don't suppose you'd stoop to anything that phoney.'

'I don't think I'd get away with it.'

Jeff's tone was philosophical. 'No, I guess in your world you have to play it straight. Anyway, doll, you might have your heartaches, but at least nobody owns you. When you want to fall for somebody, you don't have to ask Roger's permission.'

'I'm not going to feel sorry for you,' Audrey told him. 'If you really wanted to free yourself, you probably could.'

Jeff stared morosely into his empty glass. 'Certainly. With one small adjustment. I'd have to enjoy going back to work in a gas station. That's where I was when Roger placed his golden finger on my brow.'

Jeff was admitting his weakness, and the admission saddened him. Audrey forgot her own melancholy, listening to this man who was idolized by millions of women and envied by millions of men. He wasn't her idea of a man, but she felt for him the same compassion she would have extended to an animal trapped by its own weakness—especially when Jeff Beaumont addressed no one in particular and announced, 'I'm famous.'

'I guess you are.'

'Lousy with money.'

'I'm sure of it.'

Again there was a meaningful silence, and then a dejected, almost defeated admission. 'You know something, Red? I need another drink.'

Audrey saw him leave, then return, fresh drinks in his hand. Once, twice, a third time, and finally the party ended. Dan Agnew, as high on a cloud as the celebrity with whom she had spent the evening, drove her home, saying he hoped she had had a good time, and wasn't Roger a friendly, sociable guy, and how about that Ginger Lampton! Wasn't she something . . . nothing high-hat about her, or about any of the fascinating people they had met tonight.

Dan walked Audrey to her door. There was a stiff pause during which he seemed to be debating whether or not he should kiss her good night; Audrey solved his dilemma by pushing the door open and saying, 'Thank you, Dan. I'll see you at the hospital.'

She closed the door before he had a chance to express annoyance or surprise . . . or relief. Audrey listened, hearing his footsteps recede . . . down the stairs, onto the sidewalk, toward his car at the curb. And out of my life, she thought. No one watching or listening to the dedicated young surgeon who had missed out on the pleasures life has to offer could have doubted that Dan Agnew had learned how to make up for that loss. It had only taken the right people to show him how. Roger Castle and his protégé. Audrey leaned against the door, closing her eyes painfully. Outside, a motor started up and raced down the street. In a few more seconds there was no sound but that of her own uneven breathing.

Who was better qualified than Ginger Lampton to lead Dan into that world in which Jeff Beaumont found himself caged? That world in which genuine love and real people didn't exist!

Chapter 4

On the four or five occasions during the next few weeks when Audrey West saw Dan Agnew, he was pleasant, cheerful . . . and nothing more. He was pleasant with everyone at the hospital; why should he make an exception in her case? Near the end of the third week, during a particularly hazardous operation, while Joan Hazelrigg daubed perspiration from his brow with a pad of gauze, Dan glanced anxiously toward Audrey. Above his mask, his eyes looked tired, almost bewildered. And unethically, because a scrub nurse was there to slap instruments into the surgeon's hand, not to relay personal messages, Audrey winked at him. It was a wink of encouragement, a sign of her belief that he would prove himself during the trying moments ahead.

The pause in surgery lasted no more than a second or two; the blotting of his forehead (vital, because one drop of perspiration in the operative field represented a dangerous break in asepsis), then the realization in Dan's eyes that he was sweating profusely, that he was more tense than he had any right to be. And, finally, that split-second wordless reassurance from Audrey: *I know a free vein graft is a tricky procedure. It's an amazing operation, a comparatively new one. And I know at least one older, more experienced heart surgeon who wouldn't attempt it. I've seen you do it before, Dr. Agnew. Here's a patient who hasn't a prayer if you don't do it again. But you will! I know you will!*

There was only that silent message, yet no doubt it had communicated itself to Dan. It was as though every nerve in his body had drawn reserve strength and confidence from Audrey's impetuous signal. He worked unhesitantly after that. Audrey found herself anticipating his needs, responding to his crisp requests for instruments more quickly than ever. And, like the rest of the team, she became absorbed in the amazing surgical procedure itself.

Their patient was a man in his mid-forties. Some months ago he had suffered an acute coronary attack, his third, bringing a harried and exciting career to a sudden halt. Electrocardiographic tracings revealed severe damage to the heart muscle. The diagnosis was an alarming one; arteriosclerosis of the coronary artery, which supplies blood to the wall of the heart muscle. Audrey had learned early in her nursing career that closure of this life-supplying artery, usually occurring in men during their prime of life, was a common cause of death today. And it was this knowledge that lent to the deftly played surgical drama before her an aura of the miraculous. When the operation was completed, a vein graft taken earlier from the patient's arm would connect the main artery with the venous channel of the heart muscle, improving the circulation.

'In a free vein graft, we reverse the normal flow of blood,' Dan had once explained. 'Heart veins aren't subject to arteriosclerosis.'

He had smiled then. 'It's surgery outsmarting the inevitable.'

He wasn't smiling during the time his gifted hands defied the inevitable. But neither did he show any further signs of strain or worry. When the incision that had been made between the patient's ribs was carefully sutured, a general atmosphere of satisfaction pervaded the O.R. They had all been participants in a difficult task well done, and the prevailing mood was almost one of lightheartedness.

'Pulse strong,' Dr. Blair, the anesthetist, said. 'Blood pressure 134. Considering the patient's cardiac history, I doubted he could stay under anesthesia long enough for you to finish.' He glanced up at the wall clock. 'Nowhere near two hours.'

Dr. Breen, the new resident assistant, muttered a reverent, highly unprofessional, 'Wow!'

Dan Agnew slipped out of his gloves. 'First time you've scrubbed in on a free vein graft to the aorta?'

'Yes, Doctor,' Breen said. He was an eager, deeply thoughtful newcomer to the hospital. At times his seriousness and thirst for medical knowledge reminded Audrey of Dan's. 'I understand Dr. Voss was one of the first men to attempt it.'

*　　　*　　　*

Ordinarily, Dan Agnew would have given the young resident a detailed account of that experience; more than once Audrey had heard him describe his own exultation at seeing a miraculous new operation performed by the man he idolized. Now, contrary to the spirit of camaraderie that had taken hold of the others, he only nodded wearily.

While Dr. Blair was putting away his equipment, and before the patient was moved from the table and wheeled to Recovery, Dr. Agnew waved a listless goodbye to everyone in the room, apparently including Audrey in his impersonal farewell. 'Thanks, people. I've got to run.'

It seemed to Audrey that the white-tiled room would collapse around her. 'Thanks, people!' as though he hadn't admitted, only a few short weeks ago, that he had given serious thought to asking her to marry him! And just a few minutes ago, when he had faltered, hadn't he looked to her for moral support? To her, because she understood his work, understood his devotion to surgery, understood him? 'People,' the way you might say it to a crowd of strangers!

As usual, Joan Hazelrigg caught Audrey's reaction immediately. Surprisingly, Dr. Blair sensed her depression, too. Without turning their attention from the patient, they launched a deliberately nonsensical repartee, obviously aimed at restoring the warm, winning-team atmosphere that Dan Agnew's cool exit had disrupted.

'It just occurred to me,' Dr. Blair said, his tone one of mock seriousness. 'Did you ever account for all the sponges?'

It was a tired joke; the conscientious accounting had been taken, of course, before the patient's incision had been closed.

'Darn! Forgot again,' Joan said. 'We lose more sponges that way.'

'Oh, well. The hospital can afford it,' Dr. Blair went on. 'It's what you did last week that'll get you girls in trouble some day. Remember, Audrey? After that gastric resection?'

Joan feigned a bored yawn. 'It wasn't serious. Just that we're out one laparotomy sheet.'

'And an orderly—don't forget that!'

Joan managed a quick look in Audrey's direction. 'Everybody's entitled to a few small mistakes.'

They're trying to cheer me up, Audrey thought. Knocking themselves out, trying to be funny, hoping they'll take my mind away from Dan. The least I can do, she decided, is to pretend they're succeeding. But is my love so obvious to everyone? Is my misery plain even to Dr. Blair? Maybe the orderly sees it, too!

Joan and the orderly, who was obviously enjoying the foolish banter, eased the patient onto the stretcher, Audrey assisting in the careful move. She stretched her mouth in what she hoped was a convincing smile, but the appropriate wisecrack for which she dredged her mind refused to materialize.

Finally, because they were politely waiting for her to say something, even apart from their nonsensical chatter, giving her a chance to save face and pretend that she hadn't been hurt, Audrey nodded toward their patient. 'He's a fortunate man, isn't he?'

Joan scowled. 'All patched up,' she said icily. 'That's the advantage of putting your faith in a cardiac specialist like Dr. Agnew. You get your ticker mended.' Under her breath, she added, 'Or broken. Depends on whether you're a patient or a darnfool nurse.'

Dr. Blair and the resident assistant had walked away, discreetly pretending that they hadn't heard.

*　　　*　　　*

By the end of the month, Audrey's concern over Dr. Dan Agnew had become twofold. There was the personal agony of not hearing from him, the hours of waiting for the phone to ring, the weekends without him, seeing him only in the line of duty, with only the briefest exchange of words before and after surgery. There was another worry, too, not truly concerned with her love for him, yet not wholly separated from that love, either. It was a worry that came alive gradually . . . in the operating room.

At first she thought the change in him was a product of her own imagination, or more accurately, her own bias. Dan was no longer the Dan he had been; he was barely more than a genial stranger. Wasn't that why she was seeing a stranger's hands under the glaring reflectors? Wasn't that why operative techniques that had been as familiar as his voice on the phone were suddenly different? She found herself confused by his occasional hesitancies. Though the operations and instruments required had been varied in the past, there had developed between them an almost automatic rhythm in which the knife or needle-holder required was in Dan's gloved hand in the precise instant that the hand was blindly extended. Audrey had taken pride in their often-wordless communication. With other surgeons, she was an efficient scrub nurse; with Dan Agnew, she felt that she was an extension of him. As Joan had commented once, 'The two of you together . . . you could both be deaf, dumb, and blind, and I'd let you operate on *me!*'

But now . . . no, it wasn't imagination or the fact that their personal relationship had changed. Now there was a tiredness about Dan. On more than one morning he came into the O.R. looking tired and bedraggled, deep, dark circles of sleeplessness underscoring eyes that appeared listless. He would perk up after slipping into his gown and gloves, and no one could have accused him of a careless attitude or faulty technique. Audrey decided that perhaps she was the only one who noticed those split-second hesitancies, the rigidity of his movements—telltale indications of tension and fatigue. Dr. Voss was planning to leave on a European tour shortly, completely divorcing himself from his practice. Was Dan studying late at night, worried about stepping into shoes too large for him?

And was Audrey the only one who noticed the brief pauses, the deep sighs, the momentary halts that implied indecision? It was a question she asked herself endlessly. The assisting doctors wouldn't make any comment, even assuming they had become aware of the change in Dr. Agnew. Certainly they wouldn't express even the mildest criticism in the presence of the nurses. Besides, Dan Agnew was still maintaining his enviable record, matching the most danger-fraught operations with a miraculously low mortality rate. No, there was no one who would have agreed with Audrey; Dr. Agnew remained, perhaps justifiably, the pride of Hollywood Memorial.

Joan Hazelrigg, whose tongue was often as critical as her eye was quick, made only the most circumspect references to the matter.

Helping Audrey set up for an operation that followed one of Dr. Agnew's, the chubby 'chase nurse' said casually, 'Doctor looked tired today.'

Audrey nodded, afraid to express her growing concern.

'Matter of fact, he looked beat,' Joan persisted.

'Yes, sort of.'

'Standard operating procedure lately, have you noticed? What's he doing, living it up?'

'I wouldn't know,' Audrey said. She busied herself laying out the instruments that would be needed for the ten-thirty splenectomy.

'Well, he looks like eight hours of sleep wouldn't hurt him. Brother! When he started that septal repair job the other day, he was so jittery I thought he'd pass out before the patient did.'

Defensively, although the same thought had occurred to her earlier, Audrey said, '*You* try repairing an opening in the wall between the left and right auricles. *You* do it, on a woman who's hanging onto life by a thread anyway. Tell me you wouldn't be high-strung!'

'The word I used was "jittery." '

'That's not a proper criticism.'

'Calling 'em as I see 'em, West.' Joan reconsidered for a moment, then added, 'Course I wouldn't say it to anyone but you. "Jittery" has a . . . kind of bad connotation.'

Audrey nodded again, solemnly this time.

Joan eyed her quizzically, as if seeking out Audrey's reaction. 'Meaning in no condition to operate, right?'

'Forget it, will you? Dr. Agnew works hard. He's taking over Dr. Voss' practice . . . tremendous responsibilities. Old Doc Voss probably has him boning up on case histories until all hours of the night.'

Joan shot her a disbelieving look, but she said, 'I guess so.'

'And I've told you how seriously Dr. Agnew takes his work. Practically killed himself getting through med school. Once he told me that four hours' sleep was a big deal during his internship.'

'It must still be a big deal,' Joan concluded. 'The difference being that then he used to watch operations. Now he's performing them.'

'With rather good results, wouldn't you say?'

Joan sighed, admitting that this was true, that her criticism was probably out of line. But she wasn't buying that theory about Dr. Agnew burning the midnight oil, she insisted. 'I was down in the staffcaf a couple of days ago, just a table over from him.'

'And?'

Joan colored suddenly, as though she regretted opening the subject.

'And what, Joan?'

'And he was giving a couple of doctors from O. B. a vicarious guided tour of L. A. night spots, with a Las Vegas weekend thrown in free of charge.'

Audrey hoped that her face didn't reflect her inward reaction. With an effort at indifference she asked, 'Is there a law prohibiting doctors from enjoying themselves? He can afford to have fun now . . . he went without it long enough.'

Joan waddled away from her, headed toward Surgical Supply B, apparently ready to drop the argument. 'Maybe that's why he's flipped so completely. Keep an animal chained up for ten years and then turn it loose, well, it'll run around until it exhausts itself.' Under her breath, she added, 'Especially if there's a cute lady animal leading the chase.'

She knows something I don't know, Audrey thought. Joan feels sorry for me, and whatever's on her mind, she's trying to let me know it in slow degrees, because Joanie's fond of me, and she's one of the kindest people I've ever known.

There was the sinking sensation, then, of knowing someone pities you. And that ever-present threat to the pride—who else knows you're hopelessly in love, that you've been ruled out of the competition? Who else feels sorry for you, perhaps patronizingly sorry, not sorry out of the compassion and romantic idealism that motivates Nurse Hazelrigg? *Everyone who knows me*, Audrey concluded.

She finished her shift in the operating room

mechanically, her senses dulled, an aching hardness in her throat substituting painfully for unreleased tears.

A man couldn't change this completely in one month! He couldn't consider you his closest friend, the one possible candidate for marriage, the only prospective lifemate . . and then personally and professionally reveal himself as a chill stranger.

Had she overestimated Dan's warm feeling for her? After all, he had never made any promises; he wasn't bound to her by any contract. Had she overglorified his dedication to surgery? No, that wasn't it. Joan had pinpointed the problem; Dan Agnew had been caged too long, and now he was experiencing some sort of bursting forth—a releasing period of carefree socializing, the novelty of which would wear off, after which Dan would return to his work and his old friends. (Audrey was afraid to think in terms of an 'old love.') Yes, this was the way it would be, she rationalized. She would go on loving him, and she would be patient, confident that Dan was experiencing nothing more serious than a brief, sorely needed fling.

If she didn't quite believe that pacifying excuse, it at least helped make the hours between seven and three bearable. It wouldn't do to cry during hours on duty. That was a luxury she reserved for the hours alone at home.

Chapter 5

There was a balmy evening in May during which Audrey found no time to indulge herself in self-pity. It began with the arrival of Irene's enterprising soulmate, Charlie Perkins.

Charlie had a wild curative theory to match any ailment known to man and regarded the entire medical profession as a gigantic hoax. He was given to making uninvited snap diagnoses; many a surprised stranger had been told that eating celery would cure his nervous tic and the consumption of goat's milk would cure whatever else troubled him. Charlie firmly believed, and would assure anyone who could be cornered into listening, that garlic was the only bonafide cancer preventative. If he had operated as a quack doctor, Charlie's fanaticism would have rendered him dangerous. Fortunately, his mail-order entreaties dealt with harmless foodstuffs, and most of them fell on deaf ears.

Besides, anyone seeing Charlie Perkins in the flesh, with his sparse, unmuscular frame, myopic eyes, hypertense mannerisms, blanched face, and disappearing hair, could only conclude that, if Charlie Perkins recommended something, it was, at all costs, to be avoided. He was a testimonial in reverse, the 'before' in a 'before-and-after' ad—but immensely likable in spite of his zealous, single-trolley mind.

Audrey would have found his disdain for the medical fraternity intolerable except for his personality and for the comedy relief he provided around the apartment. Irene Rafferty, in spite of her scientific training and job, regarded him as something of a dietary messiah; Audrey could never get away from the impression that Charlie had escaped from a comic strip.

This evening he and Irene were more wound up than usual; they were duplicating the cover of a Charlie-Irene collaboration titled, *Wheat Germ; Your Golden Key to a Longer Life!* Audrey made an abortive attempt to drown her misery in a TV situation comedy, but the grind-and-slap of the duplicating machine in the dining area played havoc with the sound. She clicked the set off in exasperation and started up the stairs to her room. There was *that* advantage to the duplex; she could always get away from the health fiends.

Charlie, rotating the handle of the hand-cranked machine, nodded an unsolicited agreement. 'Good idea, Audrey. TV's hard on the eyes.' He blinked, squinted to see if the last page he had turned out was properly inked. 'You've been having trouble with your eyes.'

Audrey flushed, certain that he had seen

64

them swollen from crying on more than one recent visit. She covered her embarrassment with critical sarcasm. 'Yes, *Doctor* Perkins.'

From the floor, where she sat stacking the finished pages, Irene howled, 'Was that supposed to be smart?'

Charlie rose above both criticism and defensiveness. 'Carrot juice. If I were you, I'd drink gobs of carrot juice. That's what I'd do.' He blinked behind his thick-lensed glasses (a concession to orthodoxy which they never discussed) and assured Audrey that he really had nothing against doctors and nurses. They came into the picture, Charlie explained, after a lifetime of improper nutrition had done its damage.

Audrey thought of Bonnie Castle; the sudden attack of rheumatic fever, the destructive scarring that had narrowed the vessels of the child's heart. There were thousands of critically afflicted human beings for whom surgery at the hands of a Dr. Voss or a Dr. Agnew meant the difference between painful death and joyous life. She thought of the years of study, the fatigue, the self-sacrifice, and the burning determination demanded of a man before he earned the right to add M.D. after his name! A wave of anger came over her, and suddenly it came to her that it was her own furious voice shouting, 'You presumptuous, ignorant cereal peddler! You have the nerve to look down your nose at men who can afford to forget more than you'll ever know!'

Irene was on her feet, her thin face blazing red, the horrible muu-muu contrasting screamingly with the unnatural color of her features. 'Look . . . you've no right to talk to Charlie that way!'

'I'll stop when he quits maligning a profession he knows nothing about. My profession, incidentally.'

Charlie raised his head in a flabby, placating gesture, 'Now, girls! . . .' He was an armchair fanatic, not a warrior.

'I don't blame him nearly as much as you!' Audrey cried out. 'You've been around hospitals long enough to know better.'

'Girls, you're both a little on edge.'

'I won't have Audrey insulting my friends!' Irene hurled out the heroic statement, then returned her ire to Audrey. 'Just because you're all shook up about a fickle medic doesn't mean you have to take your frustrations out on us! It's not *our* fault Agnew's chasing some flashy nightclub singer!' Irene's face assumed an even deeper shade of crimson. She had finished the sentence, but there was a wavering quality in her voice; Irene had blurted out something she would rather have kept to herself.

Audrey inhaled deeply, the air congealing in her lungs. She could pretend indifference, making them think this was no surprise to her.

But I'm not up to playing the actress, Audrey decided quickly. There was nothing to do but ask, 'And where did you pick up *that* little tidbit?'

'About Ginger Lampton?'

'Yes, Ginger Lampton.' Hearing the name, repeating it, was like a knife thrust into the ribs . . . once, twice! 'I didn't tell you about our meeting her at . . .' Audrey stopped. Though she shared the apartment with Irene, their friendship had always been rather casual, without the sort of confidences she could share with Joan Hazelrigg. Where had Irene learned about Ginger Lampton?

'I read the theatrical columns, old girl,' Irene said. Then, her temper abating as suddenly as it had flared up, she appeared embarrassed, and finally, as Audrey stared at her in bewilderment, Irene's eyes filled with tears. 'Gee, Audrey . . . that was crummy. That wasn't the way I meant to tell you about it.'

Audrey turned her back to Irene, but not in anger. 'I asked for it,' she said. And it was true. Charlie and Irene were no more deserving of her fury tonight than they had ever been. At worst, they were misdirected screwballs; at best, a pair of good eggs she could count on in a pinch. Was it their fault that she had been the last person to learn the truth? Or because everyone around her knew that Dr. Agnew and Ginger Lampton were a twosome, that her own love for Dan was

67

something pitiable in their eyes? How immature to take out her frustrations on innocent bystanders!

'I'm sorry,' Audrey muttered. 'Can we forget it?'

Irene nodded, and the phone rang, sparing all of them a sticky round of apologies and probably disappointing Charlie Perkins, who relished opportunities to make long, flowery speeches on the subject of a friendly atmosphere as related to the digestive system.

'That'll be for you,' Irene said. Her one possible caller was in the room.

Audrey nodded. The phone rang again, and she crossed over to the secretary, lifting the receiver without feeling the glow of expectation that had always accompanied that act. It wouldn't be Dan.

It wasn't. Audrey's listless, 'Hello' was followed by a vaguely familiar, inquiring voice. 'Hello. Is this Miss West?'

'Yes.'

'This is Richard Voss, Audrey.'

'Oh . . . I thought I recognized your voice, Dr. Voss.'

There was an amused chuckle on the other end of the line. 'Old and crochety, eh? And before you become convinced I'm suffering from senile hallucinations . . . I didn't call for a date, young lady!'

Audrey laughed; the old surgeon's self-deprecating good humor was infectious. 'Mrs.

Voss should be happy to hear that, Doctor.'

'Yes. Matter of fact, she's sitting right here in my study, and it was her idea to call you, dear. We're . . . a bit worried.'

'Can I help?'

Now the frivolous introduction was replaced by a quiet, concerned tone. 'We thought you might be able to. When Mrs. Voss remembered you're the only girl Dr. Agnew's ever . . . talked about, she thought . . . that is, we wondered . . .' Dr. Voss paused a moment, then plunged into his problem abruptly. 'You're close to Dan. I don't know what's come over him. We can't seem to communicate any more. We thought, if you could convince him that . . .'

Audrey interrupted. 'Dr. Voss, if he's making a mistake, he's not doing it with my help.'

'But he's serious about you. You'll be able to reason with him!'

Apparently Dr. Voss didn't read the gossip columns, either. 'Doctor, I don't see Dan any more. Except at the hospital.'

The momentary quiet that followed could have been interpreted as a stunned silence. And then it became clear that Dr. Voss hadn't been referring to Dan's exhausting new night life; that he was, in fact, completely unaware of it. 'You might talk to him at the hospital, then. He has a great deal of respect for your opinions, young lady. I ought to know that. If

69

he's too busy reviewing laparotomy techniques to spend any time with you, then it's more serious than I supposed.'

'Too busy doing *what?*'

'Hasn't he told you? Dan's talking about expanding into a general surgical practice. He's insisting that cardiac surgery is too limited a specialty! Limited . . . with research opening new horizons every day! With men like himself standing on the threshold of conquering the nation's number-one killer! At a time when heart surgery needs aggresssive, dedicated . . .' Dr. Voss' voice rose during the impassioned protest, quavered, and then dropped to the gentle quality more typical of him. 'Forgive me, my dear. I think of Dan Agnew's potential and I get carried away.' Almost sheepishly, the old man explained, 'Mother's giving me her "simmer down" signals.' But this time, when he laughed, the sound rang hollow.

Audrey searched for a reply. Animated voices from the other end of the room distracted her for a moment; someone had apparently joined Charlie and Irene. What was there to say? Could she disillusion the great surgeon completely? Tell him the promising young doctor he had guided, the man he had selected to carry on his specialized scientific crusade against death, was 'expanding his practice' to a round of dates with Roger Castle's ex-girl friend? No

70

pain can equal that of a shattered dream, and no one who experienced it could justifiably inflict it upon another. 'I'll do what I can,' Audrey said. 'But please don't count too heavily on my influence, Doctor.'

He thanked her, apparently assured that one word from Audrey West would restore Dan Agnew to the logical role of his successor. Then he added, 'Mother's saying something in the background. Just a minute, please.'

Audrey listened to two undecipherable conversations at the same time—one in the Voss residence, one behind her back, neither penetrating the fog. *Dan's in love with someone else. Dan's giving up the opportunity he worked for so desperately. Why?*

Dr. Voss was back on the line. His wife, he said, hoped Dan and Audrey could have dinner with them soon; Mrs. Voss had heard so many complimentary things about Audrey from the young surgeon that she was determined to meet 'that lovely young girl of Dan's' before leaving on the forthcoming European tour.

'I'd love to, of course,' Audrey said uneasily. 'But you'd better talk to . . .'

'Then it's settled. We'll get Dan to set the evening.' Dr. Voss' enthusiasm was touching. 'He's busier these days than the rest of us, so we'll leave it up to him.'

They exchanged goodbyes, the doctor's

ringing with renewed confidence and Audrey's a disheartened attempt at reflecting the elderly surgeon's enthusiasm.

She had barely replaced the receiver when the now-recognizable voice of the visitor floated toward her:

'My aunt in Newark drank eighteen cups of coffee a day. Died at the age of one-ought-one, and, sweetheart, she looked better at her wake 'n all three of us combined look right now!'

Audrey wheeled around in time to catch the horrified gasps of Charlie and Irene and to see the pleased, if somewhat bleary smile on the handsome face of Jeff Beaumont. He was grinning at the consternation he had caused, standing there with a mammoth bouquet of white roses in his arms. Dark glasses, a rather disreputable pair of denim work pants, and a gray sweat shirt had evidently been pressed into service as a disguise—a successful one, if Irene's next remark was any indication. 'On the coffee issue we emphatically disagree with you, Mr. Feebish!'

Jeff had turned his attention to Audrey. As she approached the trio, he extended the bouquet, accompanying that gesture with a slightly unbalanced bow. 'Snow Whites for Rose Red! Compliments of Horace J. Feebish.'

Still reeling from her past two conversations, Audrey blinked her eyes. Then, accepting the flowers, she said, 'Be sure to thank him for me. How are you, Jeff?'

'Ah-ah-ah!' He held a waggling forefinger to his lips. 'Don't expose me to the multitudes.' Feigning a surreptitious glance around the room, he slurred, 'T'night I'm incognito, incommunicado, an' . . . insufferable. Right, doll?' He grinned again at Irene.

'No one's going to mob you here,' Audrey assured him, going through the round of introductions and seeing Irene's eyes widen and Charlie's mouth fall open upon discovering that this faintly tipsy intruder was a famous celebrity.

'I'm hiding, I'm hiding, and no one knows where,' Jeff assured them all.

Irene led him to a comfortable seat while Audrey found a vase for the flowers, filling it at the kitchen sink and hearing Charlie's voice from the living room, launching into an obsequious assurance that Mr. Beaumont's coffee-drinking aunt might have had an exceptional constitution, but the average person . . .

Jeff, feeling no pain, was enjoying the conversation immensely. 'Wheat? Is wheat good? Barley?'

'All whole grains,' Irene said emphatically.

'Oh, that's comforting to know. I practically live on grain,' Jeff told them solemnly.

'You're very wise,' Charlie nodded.

'Nothing like whole grain.'

Before the health addicts could go into ecstacies, Audrey returned to the living room with the vase of roses. 'He means after it's been mashed and fermented,' she said. 'Right, Mr. Feebish?'

Jeff laughed delightedly, but the leg-pulling had done nothing to relieve the awkward situation. Charlie merely looked bewildered. Irene sat tight-lipped, eyeing the famed entertainer with the scorn she usually reserved for unbleached flour.

Uncomfortable, with too much on her mind to be of any value to the conversation, Audrey wished Jeff would leave; coming to call on her in his condition was hardly flattering. An evening in this stilted, mismatched company was impossible to contemplate, and certainly she couldn't go out with Jeff. Why was he here?

He might have come, Audrey decided, because he needed a respite from the *papier mâché* world in which he felt trapped. Jeff had been kind enough to ease her out of an embarrassing situation at their first meeting. If he felt the need to come here, to lose his identity for a few hours, she owed it to him to be sympathetic. And sympathy was the only word for it, because Jeff's potent charms were strangely lost on her; she looked upon him now as an engaging, wistful, and thoroughly mixed-up older brother.

With Audrey depressed, Irene hostile, Charlie befuddled, and Jeff Beaumont oblivious to all of their reactions, the gaps of utter silence grew increasingly longer. Irene finally broke the impasse by reminding Charlie that they had work to do. They excused themselves, retiring to the dining area and closing the sliding door between the two rooms, so that a few minutes later there was no indication of their presence except the persistent slapping sound of the duplicating machine.

'I'm afraid celebrities don't impress them very much,' Audrey apologized. Jeff's pleasant indifference erased the weight of her personal problems. Seeing the relaxed manner in which he occupied the sofa opposite her chair, she found herself smiling. 'Maybe they still think you're only Mr. Feebish.'

'There are times, Red, when I wish they were right.'

'Times like?'

'Like when I get fed up to here with fans, phonies, and kissing Roger's gold-plated foot.' Jeff grinned. 'Like when I can dress like a hod carrier and sit around shooting the breeze with a girl who doesn't have ulterior motive number one. We went all through this bit before, Red. Tonight it's even better because of those two.' He thumbed toward the dining room. 'Didn't even ask for my autograph. Whatever they're peddling, remind me to buy some.'

'They're selling the long, healthful life.'

Jeff's features twisted into a brief wry expression. 'I'll never make it.'

'You could give up a bad habit or two,' Audrey suggested.

'Honey, if I gave up lushing, I wouldn't be able to drown out the *reasons.*'

'Reasons? I don't follow you, Jeff.'

'Reasons why I'm liable to lead a short, unhealthy life, doll. Bad case of Rogeritis.'

He was sober enough, Audrey was certain, to make himself clear. 'Jeff, please talk sense. I honestly don't know what you're talking about.'

' 'Member what I told you about too much knowledge? Not healthy.' He sighed, shaking his head as if to dislodge a disturbing thought. The silly, devil-may-care attitude had fled, replaced now by a moody hesitancy, as though there was something preying upon his mind, something he needed to release by talking, yet something he was afraid to express.

Audrey told him as much.

Jeff was silent for a few moments, his thumb and forefinger rubbing against his eyelids. When he spoke again, he was completely lucid. Somehow a more serious cloud had obscured the alcoholic fog of casualness. Perhaps the easy manner had been a pose; now he sounded like a frightened stranger. 'O.K., you want to know what's

76

bugging me. You're sharp enough not to repeat it. That's more than I can say for people I've known a lot longer than I know you, Red.' His voice dropped to a near whisper. 'I don't like my little playmate. I don't like the way he gathers his bread.'

'You mean money.'

'Big money.'

'I imagine you're talking about Roger Castle and his cut into your earnings?'

'I'm talking about Roger, all right. But his cut is peanuts compared with the main source. The clubs, the talent agency . . . that's all a respectable front. Profitable, lousy, but strictly legal.'

'What *isn't* legal, Jeff?'

He hesitated, glancing toward the adjoining room. The duplicating machine continued its rhythmic noise. 'Maryjane, H, snow, joy caps . . . lots of names for it. You probably know the technical terms, nursie. One of my best friends calls it pure Hell; Buddy had a big career in jazz 'til he got hooked. He's paying for it . . . he's a victim. The guys who run the stuff are guilty, but the Buddy's pay the price.'

'Drugs?'

'Shh! You'll wake the baby.'

Audrey lowered her voice. 'But how would you know? Assuming you were right, he'd certainly be careful . . .'

'Oh, he is, he is. But Roger has this thing about company. Loves a swingin' party, loves

77

to flash names around. So Jeff Beaumont's got to be there. I'm a fixture around the place. Sleepy, lushed-up Jeff, out like a light on the sofa. He couldn't possibly make head or tail of the phone calls that sometimes come at three A.M. Or the whispered little consultations Mr. Castle has—oh, once in a blue moon—with some of the boys. Not Jeff. No, no, no.'

'You mean you've overheard things?'

'Not often. Not clearly. Just enough. One night—this was over a year ago—Roger slapped one of his "chauffeurs" around for being careless. *Chauffeurs.*' Jeff snorted. 'That's a polite name, doll. This guy was going on about a shipment due from France . . . about how the boys in New York were getting jittery, and who was going to pick it up now that the Feds were trailing the Cado brothers? Anyway, Roger must have gestured my way . . . I was stretched out in a lounge chair near the pool. I heard Roger snarl, "Why don't you plug us into a coast-to-coast hookup, you pothead?" Meaning this hood was talking too much with a nonmember around.'

'I suppose that ended it,' Audrey ventured.

'Not quite, honey. This character'd had a few drinks himself. I heard him say something like "that plastered crooner wouldn't know what junk is if you pumped it in his right arm." The other creeps laughed. And that's where Roger let his boy have it. Smack, right across the kisser.'

'Roger slapped him?'

'Uhuh. And Roger's one third this guy's size. Then they moved into the house for the rest of the meeting. And the next question reads like a song title, honey. Does he know that I know that he knows that I know?'

Audrey pondered that for a few seconds. 'He hasn't said anything? Threatened you?'

'Nope.'

'But, of course, he wouldn't. You're a big name.'

'Big enough not to need him any more, Red. Roger's thought of that. And there's only one difference between Jeff Beaumont getting his brains bashed in and the same thing happening to some two-bit peddler. I'd have lots of wailin' teenagers at my funeral. But I'd be every bit as deceased.'

A slim suspicion that Jeff might be dramatizing himself flittered through Audrey's mind. Maybe he was replaying the plot of one of his movies. Still, he seemed to be genuinely concerned. 'Could you . . . stay out of his way? Skip some of the parties?'

'I'd be conspicuous by my absence.'

'I suppose . . . on that flimsy evidence . . .'

'I couldn't tell my tale to the Law? A couple of guys tried to beat a drug-pushing rap that way. The way I get it, they claimed Roger Castle was their boss; he'd double-crossed them, they said. And they figured that by nailing him as the brains, they'd get off easy.'

'And?'

'And nobody believed them, doll. The way nobody would believe a . . . plastered crooner. Roger's too respectable. He owns too many people in the right places. Besides, chick, I'm known for my speeding tickets.' Jeff stretched his lips in an ironic, bad-boy grin. 'If I had an "accident" some evening, no sensible cop would be a bit surprised.'

Jeff rose from the sofa, shifting back to the easygoing, self-assured characterization better known to his fans. 'So much for the shoulder-sopping routine, baby. Cry on mine anytime.'

Audrey got up and walked over to him. 'You could be wrong, Jeff. Maybe you imagined it.'

He eyed her blankly for a few seconds before he replied. 'Sure. I also imagined the Cado brothers.'

'Those were the men you heard discussed at Castle's.'

'They were the creeps who got sent up in that big drug round-up back East. Last year, remember?'

'No, I don't, Jeff.'

'You don't read the papers, Red. Probably didn't read them today, either.'

'No.'

'Monk and Eddie Cado blasted their way out of the jug.'

'Oh, yes. I heard that on a newscast. In New

York, wasn't it? There were five of them . . .'

'And they've rebagged the other three. The point I'm making is, they aren't nice kids. And it proves I didn't dream up their names . . . or their business. And remember, folks, you heard it first at one of Roger's parties!'

Jeff chucked Audrey under the chin. 'Looks like you aren't going to offer me a drink, so . . .'

'Oh, I'm sorry! We've been so busy talking. We don't drink, but . . . here, let me fix you a cup of . . .'

'Poisonous coffee?' Jeff pretended to look horror-stricken. 'No thanks, Red. Stick around here, you'll be handing me kumquat juice.'

Jeff was on his way to the door, a rather unglamorous glamour boy in Audrey's eyes; one whose success and popularity were evidently being paid for in sleepless nights. 'Why did you tell me about Roger Castle?' she asked.

Jeff shrugged. 'You've got a good ear, Red. I've got a big mouth. Now let's hope you have a lousy memory.' He opened the door. 'Say bye-bye to Princess Aloha for me.' He was referring to Irene's Hawaiian outfit, of course.

'I'll do that, Jeff.'

'And her little friend. Tell them I'm sorry if I gave them a rough go.' Jeff turned abruptly, facing Audrey. 'O.K. if I come back sometime?'

It was almost ludicrous; *the* Jeff Beaumont

asking permission to return to this colorless apartment! 'Of course!'

'If there's anything you want to know about the doc . . . I see quite a bit of him these evenings.'

Audrey avoided the searching gaze. 'I imagine you do. But I'm . . . not interested.'

Jeff shrugged again. It was obvious that she hadn't deceived him.

'It . . . while you were talking, it did occur to me that a doctor might be useful to someone . . .'

'Trafficking in drugs? No. Roger doesn't need your boy. He just happens to like Agnew. Roger's . . . let's say he has a sentimental side. Don't worry about that angle.'

'Thanks,' Audrey said. 'That's all I'd be worried about.'

'Naturally,' Jeff patted her arm. 'I didn't mean to imply you're carrying a torch, baby. We both know better, don't we?'

He lifted a forefinger, waving it back and forth slowly, signifying a casual farewell.

'Take care of yourself, Jeff,' Audrey said.

'Check.' Before he closed the door behind him, he added, 'Next time we see each other, it'll be on the sunnier side of the street.'

It was the way he said it that troubled her. Jeff used the same dubious inflection with which he had said, 'We both know better, don't we?'

Chapter 6

One week after Dr. Voss made his hopeful, naïve phone call to Audrey, she saw him again. He had said nearly a month ago that he wouldn't be scrubbing in on any more of Dr. Agnew's operations; he was genuinely retired now, only marking time until he and his wife embarked on their long-awaited vacation abroad. Yet the old surgeon appeared at the hospital early one morning, explaining to the O.R. staff that the scheduled operation to relieve a chronic constrictive pericarditis involved an old patient of his, a patient whose unique history would be included in papers that Dr. Voss planned to write now that he would have time. Dr. Agnew was expecting him, of course.

It seemed unnecessary to add that last remark, Audrey thought. As though Dr. Voss felt that he was intruding and an apology was demanded for his presence! As though Dan Agnew didn't owe him an incalculable debt! Where had he gotten the impression that he was no longer important?

Audrey's annoyance with Dan disappeared when he arrived. He was as cordial and respectful toward the senior surgeon as ever, though he appeared to be forcing an impression of freshness and brisk energy.

Whenever Dan relaxed for a moment and stopped working at this pose, the corners of his mouth revealed the same haggardness that Audrey had observed in Jeff Beaumont. It wasn't the tiredness that comes from overwork—a good night's sleep usually erased those common symptoms. It was the indelible mark of near satiation, of exhaustion from meaningless efforts. Audrey had seen the look before; the world-weariness of wealthy patients, the detached boredom of a few less-dedicated doctors. But on Dan Agnew the expression was as alien as a Halloween mask, and he must have sensed this, for in Dr. Voss's presence he wore it self-consciously . . . as though he might be ashamed. As long as he tried to pretend he was still the Dan Agnew his teacher had known . . . that Audrey had known . . . there was hope. She decided to talk to Dan at the next opportunity.

It was during the operation that Audrey wondered if it weren't too late.

The patient, an elderly man, had suffered repeated infections of the pericardial sac encasing his heart. A serious compression was being caused now by this membrane's adherence to the vital organ; surgical removal of the adherent pericardium was necessary.

Audrey had assisted in similar operations on several occasions, but she hardly considered herself qualified to evaluate the present procedure technically. Yet the delicacy required would have been obvious to a layman. And, this morning, so would the tremor in Dr. Agnew's hands.

But it was in Dr. Voss's eyes that she saw the truth. During other operations she had glanced across the table to see the old surgeon's eyes alight with pride and satisfaction—no, admiration for Dan Agnew's skill. Now the expression registered above the surgical mask was one of mingled incredulity, disappointment, and, finally, irritation.

Once, following a barely audible sigh from Dr. Agnew, Richard Voss's arm seemed to reach upward in an involuntary reflex motion . . . as though he could stand it no longer and was reaching for the knife! Only an experienced surgical nurse could have recognized that frustrated expression and motion. Dr. Voss was saying, wordlessly, 'Let *me* do it . . . please!'

Then, somehow, it was over, and the patient was on his way to the recovery room, his ordeal eased by blood transfusions, advanced techniques in anesthesia, and a gifted surgeon who was successful . . . even at his worst!

Ethics prevented any exchange between Audrey and Dr. Voss, at least none referring to the operation just concluded. But before the doctors left the O.R., it seemed to her that the oldest and wisest of them looked at her imploringly. And this time the unverbalized message said, 'He was lucky today . . . tell him that! He'll listen to you . . . he loves you!'

An old man could know so many things . . . and yet know so little!

*   *   *

It was unusual for Audrey to find herself crossing the hospital parking lot only fifteen minutes after going off duty. Ordinarily, her after-hours coffee break with Joan Hazelrigg would have delayed her at least another twenty minutes. But today Joan's dental appointment had changed Audrey's routine. Otherwise she would have missed seeing Dan Agnew walking toward her, a striking figure in a light gray, elegantly tailored suit. The morning tiredness seemed to have disappeared, replaced by a jaunty, urbane air. Recognizing Audrey, he stopped before going on into the hospital, his smile too broad and friendly to be genuine under the circumstances.

'How goes it, Audrey? They still got you coming and going?'

'No, they've . . . decided they can manage without me for a couple of shifts.'

For a moment it looked as though their meeting would end with this banal exchange. What excuse did she have for detaining him? How could she prolong the encounter when there was nothing—and everything—to say? But because there might not be another

86

opportunity to open a conversation, she said, 'You're . . . usually at your office at this time, aren't you?'

'Usually. I promised to check on a new patient of mine. Iona Lawrence.' He dropped the name casually, but namedropping it was; Miss Lawrence was a new, highly touted song-and-dance bombshell on the Hollywood scene.

'I've seen her on TV,' Audrey said. 'For a cardiac case, she seems to have unlimited energy.'

'Oh, she's not a cardiac case.' Did Dan look a trifle chagrined? If so, the reaction lasted no more than a second. 'She's in for minor surgery. You'll be seeing her in the O.R. in a day or two. In person.'

'Dan . . . couldn't . . . almost anyone? . . .'

Dan's expression chilled suddenly. 'Is this going to be a lecture on why I shouldn't accept anything but cardiac cases? If so, I've heard it from the original source.'

Audrey stared at the sidewalk, feeling the color rush to her face. 'Dr. Voss has your best interests in mind. I think you know that I do, too.'

'Then you might stop to think that I'm meeting people who can make me the top surgeon in this area. I'm getting referrals from . . .'

'The neediest patients? Or the ones you need to set you up in a Beverly Hills office?' Anger welled up inside her, and Audrey gave up hope of reaching Dan on a professional level. 'I imagine there are loads of well-heeled hypochondriacs in your new crowd. You could probably do a rushing business lifting faces and bust lines! Is that what you started out to do? All your talk about . . . coronary research . . . cutting down the blue-baby mortality.'

'Someone has to pay for research,' Dan argued hotly. 'In a few years, with a distinguished practice . . .'

'You'll have all kinds of money, won't you? You'll make Dr. Voss look like a failure by comparison.'

'Look here, Audrey! The fact that we've been good friends or that you're resentful of my new ones doesn't give you the right to question my motives. I know what's right for me. I'm still serving my profession. If I happen to . . . find myself financially successful along with that service, I can't see where you have any call to . . .'

'I'm sorry,' Audrey said quietly. 'The Dan Agnew I used to know would have understood what I'm trying to tell you.'

'For heaven's sake, let's not get sticky about it, Audrey. I'm a surgeon. I'm practicing surgery. Am I supposed to ask Voss' permission . . . or *yours* . . . whenever I accept a case?'

A horn blasted from the far end of the parking lot, and Dan turned, his face flushed with resentment. He waved at someone, then returned his attention to Audrey. 'I have someone waiting . . . promised I'd only be a few minutes,' he said curtly. Then, as Audrey stepped aside to let him go, he added, 'I'm sorry you can't appreciate progress when you see it. As an old friend, I would have expected you to be pleased.'

'Congratulations,' Audrey said. The bitterness in her voice could only aggravate him, but there was no point in pretending that she was anything but disgusted with the change in him.

'Audrey, I'd like you to see this reasonably, without . . .'

'You were right, Doctor. It's not my business . . . it's your career,' she told him, walking away quickly, before the tears spilled over and made her look foolish.

Dan seemed reluctant to let it end there. 'We'll talk about it someday when we have time,' he called back to her. 'We'll have a drink together, and I'll explain it to you.'

She didn't answer, knowing that anything she said she would regret. A nurse didn't tell a doctor that having a drink was the last thing he needed, or that there was nothing left to explain. Now the choice between dedication and dissipation was his own; she was excluded completely from Dan's present and his future.

She walked toward her parked car with a heaviness of heart, a hopeless sense of loss that she had experienced only once before . . .

coming home from another hospital after learning that neither of her parents had survived a freeway crash that had killed two others and injured three more. Then, however, there had been an escape from the terrible desolation; seeing the life-saving attempts of those doctors and nurses had given her a purpose in life. Against overwhelming odds, she had watched them keep trying . . . and though they had lost their battle, they had lighted a spark inside a bereaved sixteen-year-old girl. Having lost these two loves forever, Audrey was not completely lost herself, for she had discovered where she belonged; her decision to become a nurse had been made, ironically, in the presence of nurses whose efforts death had defeated.

Somehow the loss today was more cruel and complete. Her parents survived, strong and unchanged in her memory. But Dan . . . Dan was only a shadow now, and her own life, without him, had no substance. Oh, yes, she would continue to have value; the shortage of nurses accentuated her importance more each day. It wasn't enough, though, to be needed. You had to love and be loved. For her there was only the ghost of a man who had deserved her love, her respect, her adulation. And as she made her way across the bright, sun-filled parking area, a deep gloom possessed her. This death in life—she knew it irrevocably now—was the most sorrowful death of all.

And if that realization had not been heartbreaking enough, the occupant of the flashy yellow sports car parked only a few feet from her more austere sedan delivered the final blow. The girl behind the wheel must have seen Audrey talking to Dan; she had honked her impatience only a few moments before. But as Audrey approached the row of cars, Ginger Lampton stared cooly in an opposite direction. Either she didn't remember their meeting at Roger Castle's, or she preferred to ignore Dan's lesser acquaintances.

The snub served to emphasize Audrey's exclusion. For a few minutes she sat behind the wheel of her own car, afraid to start the motor, afraid to leave the lot and plunge into the heavy afternoon traffic; the uncontrollable tears were her own problem, not a hazard to be inflicted upon other drivers and pedestrians. Yet the thought of sitting there, waiting until she was calm enough to drive, was appalling. Dan would come out of the hospital soon and see her here. He would feel sorry for her; he would tell Ginger about the episode. Together, they would dismiss Audrey West as one of those pathetic, idealistic, overly romantic, impractical . . .

Audrey pulled the keys from the ignition abruptly, returning them to her handbag. She daubed at her eyes with a fresh tissue, then got out of the car. She walked toward the hospital, unmindful of Ginger Lampton, who would probably assume that she was following Dan.

Afternoon visiting hours were not yet over, and the main foyer of the hospital was a busy place. Audrey cut across a corner of the first-floor waiting room, past the gift and flower shop, down the short corridor to the elevators.

When something is over, you let it go completely. You don't stand beside an operating table with a shadow, seeing your love die a slow and agonizing death.

Hollywood Memorial was built into a hillside, and so there were two levels below the main floor. Audrey took the elevator to the level immediately below. A long walk down a wide, dimly lighted, marble-floored hallway led her to a door on which was lettered, SUPERVISOR OF NURSES.

Minutes later, the white-haired, matronly super who sat behind a desk in an inner office sighed her resignation and addressed Audrey. 'Well, you know what you're doing, Miss West. And I'm not one to complain when a nurse requests the eleven-to-seven shift. I was only trying to point out that your experience is best utilized on the morning shift . . . when most operations are scheduled. O.R.'s an emergency room during the night shift.'

Audrey nodded. 'I know, Mrs. Thatcher.'

The super eyed her querulously over steel-rimmed glasses. 'You're going to be missed by a number of surgeons. They get used to working with an alert scrub.'

'I'm sure I can be replaced, Mrs. Thatcher.'

The ruddy-faced matron sighed again, shuffling through a case of file cards. 'We can all be replaced, my dear. What we like to hope is that we'll be missed.' She clucked her tongue, shook her head disparagingly, and, after a brisk interval of paperwork, told Audrey that the requested change would be effective in two days. 'I s'pose you have your personal reasons,' Mrs. Thatcher said, not unkindly. And then, in a more confidential tone, 'If I had my choice, you couldn't get me off that morning shift. Did you know Iona Lawrence is scheduled for Friday morning? Miss Ortiz on the fourth floor told me at lunch. It's nothing serious, thank goodness. Isn't she the most adorable thing you've ever laid eyes on? And you'd get to meet her . . .'

'In person,' Audrey muttered.

'What's that?'

'I meant . . . I'm not impressed by big names, Mrs. Thatcher.'

'Oh, we all are, my dear! Why, when I read where one of our own doctors is going to marry Ginger Lampton! Now, you'll admit that's exciting news, Miss West. You've probably worked for Dr. Agnew time and again!'

The small, windowless room threatened to close over her. Audrey clutched the polished wooden arms of her chair, struggling for control. 'I don't . . . read the gossip columns. I . . . don't expect to be working for Dr. Agnew again.'

Mrs. Thatcher's eyes widened with incredulity, and it was plain that apart from her no-nonsense supervisory position, her existence was a series of vicarious pleasures centering around people she knew and people she could only dream of knowing. 'Everybody upstairs is talking about it,' she said. 'One of our own doctors marrying Ginger Lampton! Why, you're the first person I've talked to who hasn't been interested.'

Audrey accepted the transfer form with a quiet 'thank you.' Only two more days on the seven-to-three shift in O.R., and then the possibility of seeing Dan Agnew again would be practically nil. 'No, I . . . guess I'm not interested at all,' she said.

And then she hurried out of the office before Mrs. Thatcher could recognize it as a lie.

Chapter 7

Spring blended into summer imperceptibly. For Audrey there was no more difference between the seasons than there was between days and nights, or between one day and the next.

Since she had gone to work on the night shift, her life had assumed a strange sense of unreality. She found herself disoriented in time, sleeping fitfully during daylight hours, moving zombilike through nights at the hospital, all of it dreamlike and alien.

Her eleven P.M. to seven A.M. tour of duty was shared by several taciturn nurses who had apparently chosen the night shift because they liked silence. The resident doctors in charge were either rushed by emergencies, or catching up on their sleep in the doctors' lounge during the intermittent periods of quiet—and the interns unlucky enough to pull all-night schedules gave up their efforts to impress Audrey as soon as she made it clear that their attentions would not be encouraged. Lack of communication made the night shift a dismal period. It was made bearable only by the challenging, unscheduled cases that found their way to the O.R.—everything from common attacks of appendicitis to a full gamut of emergencies caused either by accident or design. Audrey gave herself fully to their services, for work absorbed her thoughts; work left her no time to remember.

In between, she would miss even the silly arguments with Charlie Perkins and Irene; she rarely saw them now, except on her unpredictable off nights. Joan Hazelrigg's sensitive and sympathetic ear was absent, too, and though Audrey had never known him as a close friend, the knowledge that Dr. Voss was somewhere overseas and beyond reach saddened her, perhaps because he had been her last link with Dan Agnew.

She could not say that she thought of Dan, or that she didn't think of him. He was never mentioned, for there was no one with whom she could discuss him. But, consciously or not, he was ever-present; often, she would awaken to see bright sunlight pouring into her room, realize that she had been asleep no more than an hour or two, and then remember that she had been dreaming about him. Some of the dreams were wishful, others more harshly realistic. In neither case was it possible to sleep again.

And there was the recurring nightmare in which she assisted Dr. Dan Agnew in the operation on Roger Castle's little girl; Audrey would wake up in a chilled sweat, haunted for hours afterward by a scene in which Dan fumbled and floundered, finally turned to the surgical crew and cried, 'I don't know what to do! I'm not a doctor . . . *I can't operate!*'

It was a frightening dream, disturbing her sleep in a variety of shocking versions, and Audrey decided to force the actual approaching operation out of her conscious mind. Dan would be prepared for it. Dan had proven himself time and again. And the bad dream was easily explainable: Roger Castle, and anyone connected with him, had become an aggravating symbol to her. *Let Ginger Lampton worry about Dan Agnew's success or failure. Worrying about him was the province of a wife-to-be, not a scrub nurse he had discarded.*

Over and over again, Audrey reminded herself, 'I'll never see him again. I don't ever *want* to see him again!' hoping that if she repeated it often enough, she might come to believe it was true.

*   *   *

Audrey saw Dan Agnew again early in July . . . under circumstances that made the repeated nightmares pale by comparison.

Technically, her meeting with him began while she was taking her three A.M. coffee break in the fourth-floor nurses' lounge. The small room was almost empty; one of the nurses from O.B. had removed her oxfords and was curled up in a red imitation-leather settee, dozing, occasionally stealing a sleepy glance at the wall clock. Two other R.N.'s, strangers to Audrey, worked at repairing a uniform zipper, their consultation serious and quiet. Audrey sipped her paper cup of black coffee and wondered if she would be able to concentrate on a magazine article. In the predawn stillness, the metallic voice that issued from the loudspeaker had the impact of a clanging firebell.

'Dr. Ostrow report to Emergency Service, please. Dr. Ostrow.'

Audrey had a moment in which to wonder why the surgical resident in charge should be called to Emergency before the expressionless voice intruded upon the silence once more: 'Dr. Anderson, Dr. Pokorny. Emergency Service, please. Dr. Anderson . . . Dr. Pokorny . . .'

She recognized the names as those of interns assigned to surgery. One of the zipper-repairing nurses said to no one in particular, 'Street fight, I'll bet. Buncha winos had it out on Western Ave.'

'Must be,' the other replied indolently. 'It probably looks like a sewing bee down there—all that surgical talent.'

The girl on the settee mumbled, 'Why can't everybody be quiet?'

There was silence for about five minutes, and then the loudspeaker came to life again.

'Miss West. Miss West report to Surgery.'

Audrey set her coffee aside and rose quickly.

'Must be bringing the winos up to the O.R.,' one of the nurses said. 'You'd think they'd let you finish your coffee, right, hon?' She apparently didn't expect an answer to the flippant question, returning to her tugging project. Audrey hurried out of the room.

The O.R. was a hive of activity. The nurse in charge, Mrs. Flournoy, and one of the elderly chase nurses were busy setting up, the latter breaking open a prep tray on the Mayo stand.

Mrs. Flournoy never wasted words, 'You're scrubbing, Miss West. Stat.'

Audrey hurried toward the scrub sinks, finding the charge resident already there.

'I heard them calling you to Emergency, Dr. Ostrow,' Audrey said.

'I've been there and back.' Dr. Ostrow spoke without pausing in the systematic routine, scrubbing to his elbows, then downward with a vigorous motion that somehow failed to match his unsmiling, perpetually heavy-lidded eyes. 'Guy got himself carved up. Two lacerations in the chest . . . one in the shoulder. Deep one in the gut.'

Audrey made a wincing face.

'Whoever did it missed his calling. Talk about clean cuts . . . no *débridement* necessary.'

They went on scrubbing for a few seconds, and then the resident continued, 'The attending's got to do a laparotomy —find out if the guy's hemorrhaging internally. Course, the shape he was in when I left Emergency, he won't last long enough for us to find out where the knife caught him. Say it's a vital organ; we have to suture or do a damn resection . .'

In the background, Mrs. Flournoy's voice called to someone, 'Tell him we're ready up here. Oh . . . and tell him the switchboard reached Dr. Blair. He's on his way over.'

'Blair . . . good,' Dr. Ostrow repeated. 'Boy, that fella's going to need an anesthetist who knows what's happening.'

'They must be bringing him up,' Audrey said.

'Yeah. They're really on the ball downstairs. Clamped off the bleeders, got his blood typed and cross-matched, cleaned and sutured the lesser jobs. All that before I got downstairs. Man, those rush teams down there allow five seconds to get oxygen to a patient, five more to haul out an I.V. stand and start pumping him with saline. They'll have to switch to whole blood when they get him up here.' Dr. Ostrow worked the brush around his fingers methodically. 'Course, this one brought his attending with him.'

'The patient brought . . .'

'Seems they were out on a binge together. Lucky stiff . . . at least the first aid didn't kill him. He was out with a surgeon yet! But you should have seen the mess down there! Cops all over the place, the doc yelling, "Hemostat . . . hemostat!" Not that I blame him . . . the guy was bleeding like a stuck pig—either in shock or too stoned to do any yelling himself.'

Dr. Ostrow shot a glance upward, toward the clock. 'If he's going to do this lap, he'd better get up here and start scrubbing.'

'The attending, you mean.'

'Yeah. Dr. Agnew. Say, I thought he was a heart man.'

Audrey caught her breath. 'Dr. Agnew?'

It was as though, in the shocked repetition of his name, she had summoned him. Seconds later Dan was running, half-stumbling toward the scrub sink, the stiffly starched oval of his dress shirt splattered with blood and the tuxedo trousers looking strangely out of place as he crossed the gleaming tile floor. He was still wearing the rubber gloves he had pulled on in Emergency.

Audrey heard him address Mrs. Flournoy, his voice thick and guttural: 'What's with th' lab?'

The head O.R. nurse surveyed him with a questioning expression, but her answer came forth flat and emotionless. 'He's Type A, Doctor. Six pints on the way up. We're waiting for Dr. Blair.'

'Can't wait. Time I've scrubbed, have someone else here,' Dan ordered. The steady crispness was gone from his voice, and he seemed to be making an effort to keep from slurring his words. His disheveled hair and nervous, jerky motions were understandable. But the unnatural glassiness and bloodshot appearance of his eyes had nothing to do with a hectic session in Emergency.

Dr. Ostrow had moved aside and was paying no attention to either of them as Audrey moved closer to Dan Agnew.

'Doctor . . .'

He swung his head around dizzily. Several

seconds elapsed before he recognized her. 'Audrey? Wondered . . . whatever became you.'

'What's happened?'

'Terr'ble. I wasn' inna room. Somebody broke into Roger's house . . . one min't' we're having a ball, next min't' Roger's yelling somebody tried t' kill 'im. Jeff had t' be a big hero . . . got inna way.'

'Jeff Beaumont? . . .'

'God, what's keeping that lab? Where's Blair?' Dan turned away from Audrey as though his patience had been exhausted and he could tolerate no further distractions.

It's like the nightmare, Audrey thought fearfully. *How many years has it been since he did a laparatomy? He's been drinking! He can't operate!*

Their aseptic ritual was a silent one after that. Audrey's mind gradually registered the awesome fact that their patient was not some nameless, faceless wino who'd gotten caught up in a behind-the-tavern alley fracas. *Jeff!* Jeff Beaumont, who had said, 'I'd have lots of wailin' teenagers at my funeral. But I'd be every bit as deceased.'

And Jeff's fate, if Dr. Ostrow's report had been accurate, was all but sealed. *But if he died on the table and it was reported that the operating surgeon had been in no condition to operate, Dan's career would be finished!*

Fear constricted her breathing, sticking in

102

her throat. *Say something! Talk to him! But how could you tell a highly respected surgeon that in a few minutes a man might die under his knife?*

Somehow she was gowned, masked, gloved, holding out sterilized gloves and gowns for Dr. Ostrow and for Dan Agnew, aware that Dr. Blair had materialized and was part of the scene for which hurried, half-whispered instructions and the rustle of sterile gowns provided a suspenseful background.

And then two R.N.'s from Emergency were wheeling Jeff Beaumont into the room, one of them seeing that the I.V. stand moved along in conjunction with the wheeled stretcher, with the boyish, fresh-faced intern named Anderson supervising the journey. Young Dr. Anderson, immaculate in whites, his thin figure almost but not quite obscuring the brilliant red spot staining the patient's cover sheet.

It wouldn't take much to put Jeff to sleep. Dr. Blair was less concerned with anesthesia than with the mingled oxygen needed to keep the still figure alive. Yet Jeff was not wholly unconscious. In the second before the anesthetist placed the mask over his face, Jeff's dazed eyes settled themselves on Audrey, and his blood-drained lips strained to make out a single sentence.

'It's going to be all right, Jeff,' Audrey whispered.

Did any of the others hear him? For a moment, it seemed incredible that she had heard the unintelligible words herself:

'Red . . . tell 'em . . . wasn't . . . Cado. Chauffeur . . . Rog . . . slapped 'round. For . . . same reason.'

Senseless words, yet they had been wrenched out of an agony only superficially numbed by drugs.

Think! What is he trying to tell you?

. . . Jeff floating in that nether world between painful consciousness and induced sleep . . . the routine shaving and cleansing of the operative field . . . gentle hands conscious of the deep, ugly laceration beside which the surgical incision would be made . . . draping . . . the laparotomy sheet . . . the towels . . .

What was Jeff trying to say?

It came to Audrey in quick, disconnected flashes. What was Dan's version? Roger claimed someone had tried to kill him. Cado? *Cado!* One of the Cado brothers, escaped from that prison in the East! And Jeff had tried to play the hero? *Jeff, who despised Roger Castle, standing between the man and his would-be assassin?* No one who knew Jeff Beaumont could believe that!

And who had been 'slapped around' by Roger? His chauffeur. What had Jeff said? 'Chauffeurs. That's a polite name, doll.' *One of Roger's thugs. One of Roger's thugs had stabbed . . . Jeff . . . 'for the same reason' Roger*

104

had slapped him around more than a year ago; Jeff had heard something Roger didn't want him to hear!

Suddenly there were countless, urgent reasons for keeping the knife out of Dan Agnew's hand! Jeff had to live, not only because he was a human being, not only because she was terribly fond of him, but because those few barely coherent words would not be enough to indict the man who had wanted him out of the way!

Unethical, unprecedented, insane! Audrey turned to the operating surgeon at her side. 'Dr. Agnew . . . you can't!'

Over the wrinkled green mask, Dan's eyes narrowed. The softly hissed words could not have been heard by the others. 'Mr. Castle's responsible for him . . . won't let anyone touch him but me.'

A blind desperation seized her. 'Dan! Castle wants him to die! You don't know what you're doing! Oh, Dan . . . please!'

Mrs. Flournoy must have heard her then. 'Miss West!'

The cryptic warning hung suspended in the air as Dan Agnew pushed past Audrey, his eye scanning the instrument table that had been moved in over the patient's feet.

Audrey heard her own terrified whisper as if from another room. Or perhaps she only said it to herself. 'Dan, you'll be finished! If he dies . . .'

He must have heard her. Perhaps the grim warning contained in her words had sobered him. Dan's order was clear and uncompromising:

'Scalpel!'

It had begun, and whatever she said now would only delay the slim hope that surgery held out for Jeff Beaumont. Audrey slapped the knife into Dan Agnew's waiting hand.

The others were aware. Dr. Blair, Mrs. Flournoy, the chase nurse, Dr. Ostrow, the intern. Their silent breath and watchful eyes revealed that they were aware. Dr. Agnew had no business with a knife in his hand!

Except for the wheezy, belabored breathing of the patient, the room held no sound as Dan traced the line of his incision, delineating it lightly with the faintest scratch, then cutting firmly and unhesitatingly into the living flesh. Fear had sobered him. Fear and a resurgence of the responsibility ingrained in him. It was a clean, sure cut!

Audrey's breath accelerated. Surely everyone in the room was conscious of her audible heartbeat.

She tried breathing deeply, slowly, to calm herself, but the pounding of her pulse quickened as a rush of blood from the patient's abdominal cavity confirmed Dan Agnew's fear of internal hemorrhage. She responded automatically to Dan's terse orders, pouring saline and antibiotic solution into the abdominal cavity, filling his demands for clamps, for sponges, and finally . . . sutures. Sutures, because a lacerated spot in the intestine had been located. Dan worked soundlessly, his determination evidently battering down the desperate attack alcohol had waged upon his senses.

Swift, yet painstaking stitches. Then Dr. Blair's tense and depressing report:

'He's not exchanging very well . . . his tidal volume's bad.'

Jeff's faulty respiration was only the forerunner of shock.

Dan's eyes remained fixed on the needle in his hand, tracing its painstaking motion.

'Pulse is rapid . . . thready.' The anesthetist's tone had a questioning, foreboding quality now.

'Blood pressure?' Dan's gaze didn't swerve.

'Zero over zero.'

Audrey could have verified the report by the patient's extreme pallor, the bluish-gray color of his lips.

Dan Agnew worked feverishly now. Simple procedure; find the laceration, suture it, close him up.

Simple procedure! If he can stay alive long enough for you to finish what must be done!

Dr. Blair's concern cut across the table. 'I'm not getting any pulse.'

Audrey's teeth clamped against her lower lip. *Crazy, misplaced, uncourageous Jeff. Don't die! Please don't die! . . .*

'I can't get his pulse, Doctor. Can you feel a pulsation?'

Dan Agnew's left hand found the aorta. 'It's faint. Thready.'

'But you get it?'

'Yes. B.P. ?'

'Still zero over zero.' Dr. Blair held a frozen position for a moment, then said, 'I'm getting a pulse now. Erratic . . . rapid.' A long pause. 'Respiration still shallow.'

Minutes later, with the sponges accounted for and the rubber drain tubes in place, Dan Agnew sutured the incision. Oxygen, whole blood, and an even break were all they could count on now. But the certain death threatened by internal bleeding was behind them now. Jeff Beaumont was left in the hands of Dr. Blair and God.

It took a while to restore the O.R. to its previous condition. When she had completed her tasks, with the help of Mrs. Flournoy, the circulating nurse, and an orderly, Audrey left the table to look for Dr. Dan Agnew.

He was standing in a bleak corner of the room, tugging aimlessly at his gloves, his face turned sightlessly toward the wall.

Audrey moved to within inches of his dejected back. 'I'm sorry, Dr. Agnew. I shouldn't have . . .' Tears choked back the rest of the sentence and she waited. And what am I waiting for, she wondered? For his anger?

108

For his condemnation? *I told him he couldn't operate!*

A long time later, Dan's hoarse reply told her that there was no room in him for anger or criticism. 'I didn't deserve to save him,' he said quietly.

Dan had managed to remove his right hand from the talcum-lined glove, and now his palm and fingers pressed slowly across his face. 'What was I thinking of, Audrey? My God, how many times do I rate being this lucky?'

Somewhere behind them, the intern named Anderson said, 'You know who that was?'

'Use present tense, please.' That was Dr. Blair's voice. 'We're taking him to the Recovery Room, not Pathology.'

'That's Jeff Beaumont!' Anderson went on. 'Now, tell me why somebody like that would want to get mixed up with hoods. I saw a couple of them downstairs . . . outside Emergency. You'd have to be some kind of a nut to get involved with that element!'

Dan Agnew didn't turn around, and perhaps Audrey only imagined that his shoulders were shaking. It was quite obvious that he wanted to be alone, and a short time later Audrey left the operating room to complete her interrupted coffee break. Jeff Beaumont was still alive when the doors swung shut behind her.

Chapter 8

Five minutes later, Dan Agnew came to the opened doorway of the fourth-floor nurses' lounge. He looked pale and shaken, but there was a quiet humility about him that was hearteningly familiar.

'Audrey? . . .'

She had been sitting near the door, reviewing the cataclysmic hours since Jeff had been brought into the hospital. Now she looked up to see Dan standing hesitantly in the corridor, still wearing the surgical jacket above the trousers of his tux, a sheepish expression on his face.

'Audrey, do you have a minute?'

She rose to join him out in the hall. 'Is there something I can do?'

'Castle and . . . some other people are in the waiting room. I was wondering if . . . you'd like to come with me while I give them my report.' It was an unheard-of request, and Dan must have realized that, because he explained, 'You might be able to fill in . . . some of the details.'

Audrey nodded. It was too much to expect Dan to admit that the experience in Surgery had drained him, that he needed her moral support. 'If you say so, Doctor.'

He grimaced, a pained, guilty imitation of a

smile that passed over his face only briefly.

They said nothing to each other during the long walk to the fourth-floor waiting lounge where Roger Castle, two of his 'boys,' a yawning Ginger Lampton, and two uniformed police officers waited for word about Jeff Beaumont.

'Listen, it's gettin' so a guy ain't safe nowheres,' Roger Castle was saying. His tanned, fleshy face was a map of perspiration rivulets. Once in a while he swiped at the moisture with an agitated gesture, mopping his forehead with a sogging, monogrammed handkerchief. 'A sweet guy like Jeff! You know anybody in this whole country'd wanna hurt a sweet guy like him?'

Ginger Lampton dabbed at her eyes. She had been crying; mascara smudges underscored her eyes, and the long vigil had wreaked havoc upon her theatrical charm. She would have threatened any news photographer who tried to take a candid picture of her.

'You say he got through the operation O.K.?' Roger asked for the third or fourth time.

'Better than we expected,' Dan said. He was being noncommital, Audrey noticed. If anything, he sounded negative. 'But, as I told you, his condition's critical. Frankly, I'm not holding out much hope.'

Yet on the way to this meeting, Dan had

given Jeff a better than fifty-fifty chance for recovery!

Ginger Lampton started to sniffle audibly, and one of Roger Castle's 'chauffeurs' muttered, 'Jeez!'

'Don't get me wrong,' Roger Castle said, the effort at sincerity thickly laid on. 'I ain't thinkin' about what this is gonna cost me in contracts. What's money? It's the way I feel about this guy. They di'n come no better. An' you figure he got right in the way . . . took a knife that crazy hophead meant fer me. What a guy!'

Roger was talking as though Jeff were already dead, and Dan Agnew was saying nothing to correct the impression.

One of the policemen directed a few questions to Dan. Had the doctor seen Eddie Cado? Could he identify the attacker?

Dan corroborated Ginger Lampton's story; after Roger's excited shouts, a number of the guests had looked past the patio to see a short, swarthy man run from the direction of the French windows that opened onto Roger's office, across the lawn and toward the exit gate. In the excitement over Jeff Beaumont, no one had thought to chase the assailant.

Apparently satisfied, the officers took their leave, one of them reminding Dan that they would want a statement from him. Not immediately, of course; he was too busy with his patient; but they'd be in touch.

Dan waited until the elevator had taken the policemen off the floor. And it struck Audrey that he was no better an actor than Roger Castle, because when he asked the latter, 'Exactly what did happen, Roger?' Dan's attempt to sound casual rang as phoney as Roger's expressions of concern for Jeff.

But Roger had probably repeated his tale to reporters and investigators a dozen times in the past few hours. Certainly it sounded convincing! 'I'm in my office havin' a drink with Vince here'—he gestured toward the tuxedoed gorilla at his side—'Vince and Jeff. The three of us, see, just shootin' the breeze, when this nut Cado busts in t'rough the window. I got them big door windows in this room—you seen 'em, Doc. Well, this Eddie Cado, he's no good. I pick up stuff aroun' the clubs—you know, the grapevine—an' little over a year ago, I happened t' get this tip— this guy an' his brother, they're messin' around with junk! Pushin' it, know what I mean? So who needs these kinda creeps? I do what any decen' citizen is gonna do. I call the narcotics people.'

'Naturally,' Dan agreed.

Was he guessing, Audrey wondered, or was he believing this carefully rehearsed story?

'So you know the rest. They get sent up, they make a break, an' this Eddie . . . he's the nervy one; Monk, he just follows orders . . .'

'Oh, you knew them, then? I had the

impression you'd just heard about these men,' Dan said.

'Yeah, sure, they hung aroun' the place in Vegas. So you see people aroun', that's knowin 'em?'

'Can't we go somewhere and have a drink?' Ginger complained. 'We can talk at my place . . . this hush-hush atmosphere is getting on my nerves.'

'So it's a hospital,' Roger growled. 'You want somebody blowin' a hot trumpet?'

Chastened, Ginger settled for glaring at him surreptitiously.

Roger's recital was uninterrupted from that point on, covering the demand for money from a vengeance-bent drug addict, his refusal, then reaching for the phone to call the police, and his horror at seeing Eddie Cado racing toward him with a long knife in his hand. 'Vince was so shocked . . . you c'n imagine. The both of us . . . we couldn' move. An' all of a sudden, there's my boy Jeff—he dives at this guy to stop 'im an' . . .' Roger's hand shot up to his eyes, pressing them shut as if to blot out a terrible sight. 'It was . . . awful.'

'I can't figure out why somebody didn't take a shot at him,' Ginger cut in. 'Vince . . .'

'I got no gun on me,' the big bruiser said flatly.

'You think we were expectin' a tragedy like this?' Roger demanded. 'Now, you take Cado, he knew he was gonna kill somebody. A con on the run—he couldn't stop an' buy no gun, no. But he had this knife, an' he was wearin' gloves, so you know this wasn't no accident.'

'Except that he got the wrong person?' Dan asked.

'Yeah. Cops don't even have fingerprints off the knife. But they got me an' Vince to witness. See, Cado must've panicked, but they'll get 'im. They'll get the lousy rat on a murder rap.'

'Jeff doesn't seem to think so,' Audrey heard herself saying. It was a resentful, defensive remark. And a stupid one. She knew it from Roger's cagey expression as he whirled to face her.

'What did 'e? . . . '

Dan jumped in quickly to cover for her. 'Miss West means that our patient showed . . . a great deal of stamina. Unfortunately, on the operating table he went into shock. There was no pulse at all.'

There was a controlled sigh from Vince, and Roger said, 'I thought . . . maybe Jeff was havin' . . . what they call hallucinations. Under the ether, don't people say a lotta crazy things?'

'He wasn't in any condition to talk,' Dan said gravely. 'I'm afraid he isn't now.'

Ginger made a sobbing noise, and in that moment Audrey felt truly sorry for her, forgetting that the honey-haired songstress was Dan's fiancée, responsible for those countless nights during which tears substituted for sleep. She's another ambitious fool, like Jeff, Audrey thought. Caught in the same trap, though probably not as aware as Jeff of its criminal ramifications, she must have shared a few griefs and complaints with that brighter star. If everything else about Ginger Lampton was artificial, those puffy, red-rimmed eyes were not.

Which made one out of three, Audrey concluded silently; one out of the visiting trio who didn't want Jeff Beaumont to die. And somehow Dan seemed to sense this, too. Otherwise why would he have made the almost funereal declaration: 'Miss West is due back in the operating room, and if you'll excuse me . . . I'm going to look in on Jeff. There's nothing more I can do for him, but . . . there'll probably be papers to sign.'

'Papers?' Roger thought for a minute. Then, apparently familiar with death certificates, he lowered his voice to a respectful murmur. 'Yeah. Terrible, ain't it? A sweet guy . . . never did nothin' to nobody. I feel like it's all my fault.'

Ginger assured him that no one thought that at all, and Roger mustn't let himself be plagued with guilt. Then, wearily, she asked Dan, 'Aren't you going to drive me home, hon? This has been gruelling . . .'

'You heard 'im. He's gotta stay. Vince'll see you get home.' Roger's irritation faded as he patted Dan's upper arm. 'I know you done all you could, Doc. You're still the greatest. When this is all over, you get a good rest . . . spend the week at my place in Palm Springs. Swim, soak in some sun, lay off the booze. I want you in shape when you operate on the kid.'

If he caught his own blunder, Roger Castle made no indication of it. Tonight, drunk and exhausted from lack of sleep, Dan Agnew had been the only surgeon he would 'trust' to operate on Jeff Beaumont. With Bonnie Castle's second heart operation on the hospital schedule, he wanted the doctor in shape!

'I'll be in good shape,' Dan assured him grimly.

'She's lookin' pretty good,' Roger said. 'Boy, there's a little doll! I was thinkin', good thing there wasn't no shootin' tonight, with her sleepin' in the house. It's a big place, y'know . . . people comin' over, that don't disturb Bonnie. But gunplay . . . that wouldn've been good.'

'No, we want her kept calm,' Dan agreed. He checked his watch, and the others took the cue, moving toward the elevator with Roger repeating that it was terrible about Jeff; Ginger was evidently too tired to protest the way Dan Agnew all but ignored her. Vince shuffled behind them, wordless.

'You buzz me, Doc, if there's anything . . .'

Roger called out as the elevator doors closed.

'You'll hear from me,' Dan promised. When they had gone, he turned to Audrey. 'We nearly put our foot into it, didn't we?'

'I did,' Audrey admitted. 'Thanks for bailing me out. I should have told you what Jeff said to me tonight. In fact, you ought to know all the things he told me. One evening, when he was in his cups.'

They started to walk toward Surgery. 'It would have helped to know. As it was, I was going strictly by intuition.'

'You don't believe Castle's story.'

'I've been around Jeff Beaumont too often. A sweet guy, he is. A hero, he's not.'

'Dan, if he doesn't make it . . .'

'He's going to make it; forget what I told them.'

'I wondered why you were so negative.'

'I don't know myself,' Dan said slowly. 'Unless . . . I was thinking someone might want to get to Jeff and finish a botched-up job. That's going pretty far, isn't it, just on a crazy hunch?'

'It's not going too far,' Audrey told him. 'I'd like to see a police guard on the floor. And I've got to tell someone what I know.'

'Someone?'

'The police.'

'Could you start by telling me, Audrey?'

She glanced toward the door to Surgery. 'I'm overdue now.'

118

'When do you get off? At seven?'

Audrey looked up to see Dan studying her face, his expression frankly plaintive. 'If you're . . . going to be here then.'

'I'll be here. Maybe we can go somewhere and talk.'

'If you like.'

'I like,' Dan said.

When she came off duty shortly after seven, he was waiting for her. He had exchanged the blood-spattered shirt and tuxedo trousers for an outfit of loose-fitting, borrowed whites. There were dark half-circles under his eyes, and he needed a shave, but his face lighted up as Audrey approached. Barring complications, he reported, Jeff Beaumont was going to recover.

Chapter 9

If the past few months had seemed unreal, and the hours after three A.M. that morning had resembled a disturbing dream, the process of fixing breakfast with Dan Agnew in her own apartment impressed Audrey as being somewhat less than believable.

Yet there he was, moving stacks of Irene's diet literature from the dining table to make room for the platter of hotcakes and sausages they had prepared in the kitchen; *Dan Agnew*

119

here, after the long, bleak absence, pouring chilled orange juice from a pitcher and saying, 'This was the best idea anyone's had since the invention of the mustard spoon.'

Audrey distributed the silverware, smiling. 'I couldn't quite imagine you walking into a restaurant in that outfit.'

'Please! Baggy whites and a beard are the hallmark of distinguished men of medicine.'

'You look more like a disenfranchised ice-cream vendor.'

'In his fat brother's uniform? Hey, the coffee's perking. Go, pot, go!' Dan sniffed the air. 'Right about now, I'd trade my degree and three years of my life for one measly sip.'

Audrey filled his cup. 'I'll remember that, Doctor.'

He was suddenly silent, ending the flippancy born of weariness. The wisecracking attempts had been forced, Audrey guessed, an antidote for this awkward situation. Perhaps Dan had a sensation of 'coming home,' here where he could relax completely after the arduous night. But he was uneasy, too, probably remembering that once he had considered spending not three years, but all the years of his life with her. And that he had nearly traded his medical degree for something about as substantial as a sip of coffee.

They ate quietly and, considering the many unspoken questions and answers darting

120

between them, ravenously. When Dan finished, he lighted a cigarette, exhaled a deep sigh of resignation, and said, 'That was great, Red.'

'When'd you start calling me "Red"?'

'Oh . . . I heard it used by a guy I know. Used to corner me at parties and talk about you.'

'Jeff.'

'Uhuh. I reacted with symptoms of Agnew's Disease. Jealousy syndrome. Cold, fishy stare and palpitations of the ego.'

'Shouldn't we call the hospital . . . see how he's progressing?'

'No, I left your phone number at the desk. They'll call me here if there's anything to worry about.' Dan eyed her over his coffee cup. 'Did you hear what I just said about my symptoms?'

Audrey nodded. 'A real jealousy syndrome is accompanied by a telephone fixation; acute nervousness of the dial finger. You didn't call Red, so apparently you'd never caught the germ. Let's talk about Jeff.'

They were silent again for a few moments, retiring to private chambers of thought. It wasn't possible simply to think of Jeff Beaumont and hope that he would recover. The subject opened a vast field of complications and decisions, and they had agreed not to discuss them until they had enjoyed their breakfast.

Dan broke the quiet. 'The meeting is called to order.'

'In there.' Audrey tilted her head in the direction of the living room. 'I've had it with being on my feet and sitting in hardbacked chairs.'

Tired, they made their way to the more comfortable room, Dan dropping to the sofa and occupying almost the same spot, in almost the same disjointed slouch, that Jeff Beaumont had the night of his visit. This was where Audrey had learned the truth about Roger Castle, and this was where she brought Dan Agnew up to date. She dredged up every detail of her conversation with the man who was at this moment fighting for his life at Hollywood Memorial. And when she had covered Jeff's statement from the operating table, she said, 'I don't know what happened early this morning. But I have a mental picture of kooky old Jeff sprawled out on another couch and being in on a dialogue he wasn't supposed to hear.'

'But they wouldn't . . . they'd find some less bizarre way to silence him! That was a vicious job, Audrey. I still don't understand why the knife didn't make a more vital connection.' He frowned, smoking purposefully, pondering the evidence. 'Besides, there was a stranger in the room. They didn't fake that; I saw the guy myself.'

'What if he came to make demands of

Roger? Broke in with Jeff in the room? That's Roger's story, isn't it?'

'Yes, but what if the things this Cado person said were . . . enough to convince Jeff that Roger wasn't any respectable citizen-informer. They were probably queasy about Jeff anyway, since that last incident. Maybe Cado named names and places. Maybe he even admitted he's worked for Roger, mixed up in narcotics.'

'Before he noticed Jeff was in the room.'

'Exactly. All right, maybe the rest of the story is true. Roger reached for the phone and Cado pulled a knife. But, Dan . . . can you see that ugly gorilla . . . what's his name?'

'Vince?'

'Can you see him getting the knife away from Cado? And Cado making a break . . . running out of the room?'

Dan emitted a low whistle. 'Brother! There's the perfect out. Kill an innocent eavesdropper and point the finger at an escaped convict. A guy who broke into Roger's place . . . maybe hung up for a connection . . . with a made-to-order emotive and weapon.'

'I don't want to play amateur detective. What I'm going to do is call the police.' Audrey hesitated. 'It's . . . not going to do you any good, Dan. Or Miss Lampton. If I'm right, the papers are going to have a field day.'

Dan stared at the carpet dejectedly. 'Sure. "Prominent Surgeon, Nightclub Star in Drug

Slaying." In headlines, all surgeons are prominent and all rising hopefuls are stars.'

'I wish . . .'

'You wish it weren't going to happen.' Dan rose, crossing the room to stand beside Audrey's chair.

The move caught her unprepared, and an extreme nervousness, mingled with a warm compassion for him, came over her. 'I don't like to see you hurt, Dan.'

He reached down to take her hand, pressing it between his palms, speaking in a hoarse voice that lacked tonality. 'You can't hurt me any more than I've hurt myself, Audrey. And don't ask me to explain it to you. I got carried away. Steady diet of bread and water, so I flipped over strawberries and cream. You can get awfully sick on a diet of strawberries and cream.'

Was he referring only to Roger Castle? The way he had jeopardized his medical career? Or to the complete package, including Ginger Lampton? He had not mentioned her; there was no reason to suppose he had made any change in his marriage plans.

Audrey drew her hand away. 'Dr. Voss was wrong—and I was wrong, Dan. No one can tell you what's best for you. I'm only sorry you're involved in something . . . vicious. Something I can't forget about.'

She got up from her chair and walked slowly to the phone, knowing that Dan's mood of regret and contrition would have made it easy for her to reach upward and find herself enclosed in his arms.

It wasn't going to be a pleasant call to make. Dan would inevitably be involved in the adverse publicity. Worse, people would be quick to jump on the bandwagon once his name was smeared. She thought of Mrs. Flournoy at the hospital, that conscientious old biddy getting in on the act, reporting that Dr. Agnew had performed a laparotomy while intoxicated—and doing it with every justification, for Dan had been wrong. From the word go, he had been wrong. But what a price to pay, now that he had seen the shallowness of his course!

'Dial the operator,' Dan was saying. 'Ask her for the police department. That's the fastest way.'

Audrey lifted the receiver. And someone knocked at the door.

'Expecting someone?' Dan asked. He had joined her, next to the secretary.

'At nine in the morning?' She dropped the receiver into its cradle and walked toward the door, opening it with the expectation of seeing the milkman, or someone selling something she neither needed nor wanted. In the next second her breath froze in her lungs.

There were two of them. Audrey recognized them as the pair that had accompanied Roger Castle the first time she had seen him at the hospital. Cold, emotionless faces set above broad, muscular bodies . . . the same flashy clothes. The spokesman addressed her in a gelid, impersonal tone:

'Miss West?'

'Yes. What is it?'

'Dr. Agnew here?'

'Yes, but . . .'

They walked past her, not actually shoving their way into the apartment, but moving like two irresistible masses and leaving no doubt that she couldn't have stopped them if she had wanted to.

Dan was approaching them, puzzled, but apparently recognizing the duo. 'Marco . . . Al . . . what goes on here? Did Roger send you?'

The darker-skinned thug kept his hands in his jacket pocket, saying nothing, his eyes sweeping the apartment contemptuously. His huskier, pasty-faced companion said, 'Mr. Castle wantsa talk t' you, Doc.'

'What about?'

'You talk to him, O.K.? Al an' me, we're only doin' what the boss says.'

Marco spotted the telephone, strode over to it, and dialed a number.

'What *is* this?' Dan asked. 'If he wants me, he knows how to . . .'

'We called the hospital. They said you're over here.' Marco had his hand cupped over the receiver, evidently waiting for someone to answer. 'It wasn't no snap, findin' out the address here.' His washed-out expression showed a sudden, faint sign of life; apparently someone had answered his call. 'Vince? Marco.' In monosyllables, he said, 'We're here . . . yeah . . . yeah, he's here. Both of 'em. O.K., I'll put 'im on.'

Surprisingly, Marco handed the receiver to Dan. 'Roger.'

Dan's side of the dialogue that followed was unintelligible to Audrey:

'Roger? What's the idea of? . . . Do I what? . . . *Certainly* I'm interested in what happens to your little girl. I'm her . . . I should what? Look, Roger, if somebody's in need of surgery, it's not going to help if I come out there with a little black bag. I'm a surgeon . . . I don't make house calls!'

'This house call he's gonna make,' the character named Marco muttered under his breath.

'Are you all right? . . . I dunno, Roger, you sound funny to me . . . No, what I'm trying to tell you is that . . . listen to me! If you've got someone there that needs an operation, get him over to Hollywood Memorial. I'll be waiting when he gets there . . . Roger? Are you still on the line? Roger?'

Dan turned to Audrey, perplexed. 'He wants us both at his house immediately. Wants me to bring surgical instruments!'

'Surgical? . . .' Audrey turned to address the

127

unwelcome visitors. 'Is he out of his mind? Does he think surgeons go from house to house with an all-occasion do-it-yourself kit under their arms? Do you know what preparations we make before? . . .'

'You ready?' Marco asked.

'Of course we're not ready!' Dan argued. 'I don't have any intention of . . .'

'You ready now?'

In the same instant that the dark-complected man purred his question, Audrey felt the hard, unmistakable thrust against her spine. Al was standing behind her. 'You still wanna argue, sister?'

'Dan . . .' Her voice emerged as a frightened whisper.

Dan's face had gone white. No one had to tell him Audrey had a gun at her back. 'Okay, we'll go along, but it won't do any good. I don't have any instruments here. I wouldn't know what's needed if they were here.'

'Wherever you got what it takes,' Marco said flatly, 'we stop there.'

They were being prodded, almost pushed toward the door, and Audrey's mind clawed at solutions. In detective thrillers, what did people do? Leave clues. Could she tell them she wanted to write a note to Irene? Or tell them the police would come looking for her if her roommate didn't find her at home? Think of something clever . . . some reference to foods that Irene wouldn't dream of touching

. . . something outlandish that would arouse her suspicions, so that . . .

'The boss is kinda in a hurry,' Marco was saying quietly. 'So what say we don't waste no more time?'

All the ingenious rescue plans collapsed like a punctured balloon. *Whatever he wants Dan to do, he won't let us go afterward. We'll be killed . . . the way he tried to murder Jeff!*

For a moment Audrey thought she might scream, or faint, or be sick. But there was no drastic relief forthcoming; she merely moved ahead of the pair, terrifyingly conscious of the steel object pressed against her back. Fleetingly, she wondered if the gun was hidden in the man's pocket, or if it would be seen by someone passing the duplex. Help had to come from somewhere. This couldn't be happening in broad daylight!

Then Marco was riffling through her handbag he had picked up from the desk. He found her key and locked up the apartment. Now there was only the faint hope that Irene would come home at noon . . . yes, on Saturday she only worked until twelve . . . and the uncleared table set for two would strike her as unusual, especially if Audrey wasn't around.

'Look, I don't need a nurse,' Dan was arguing. 'Whatever Roger wants, I'll try, but there's no point in dragging Miss West . . .'

'Where do we go?' That was Al, his breath warm against her ear. And they were on the sidewalk, incredibly in the bright sunlight, with no one in sight . . . no passing stranger who could help them.

A black Cadillac was parked at the curb. Marco opened the doors, standing by until Al had ushered Audrey into the back seat and joined her. Then, undoubtedly certain that Dan wouldn't attempt an escape under those circumstances, he walked around to the other side of the sleek sedan and took his place behind the wheel. Dan moved in beside him and slammed the door. *He's being cautious for my sake,* Audrey thought. And as the motor started up and the car eased away from the curb, the unbelievable terror of the situation engulfed her: *They'll kill us! We're going somewhere to be butchered!* She remembered the ugly slash in Jeff's belly, and a wave of fear and nausea rolled across her insides. *This doesn't make sense, Dan! This can't be happening to us!*

Al was repeating his arrogant question. 'I said, where do we go? Tell the driver, Doc. You need your tool kit, no?'

Dan gave them the address of his office, and the Cadillac swerved at the corner, turning again at the next intersection.

'If you'd tell me what it's all about, I'd know what I need,' Dan said. 'As it is, I won't have instruments for anything but minor surgery. And there's the problem of anesthesia.'

Marco steered the big car through the

Saturday-morning traffic easily. He sounded almost affable as he said, 'You talkin' about somethin' to knock a guy out?'

'It's customary,' Dan said tersely. 'Look, you fellas know what's coming off. Fill me in! I know Roger's not crazy enough to expect me to operate on his daughter . . . not at his home!'

The mute reaction was like a wall of silence; neither of Roger's 'boys' had any comment.

'All right, we'll do it the hard way,' Dan exploded. 'If one of your buddies has been winged by a bullet, don't blame me if I have to amputate with a safety razor and a pair of manicure scissors. Remember, I asked you what's happening.'

They ignored Dan as though he hadn't said a word, and he tried a new avenue. 'It's not Bonnie, is it? I couldn't possibly operate on her except in a hospital . . .'

Marco succumbed, though he had probably been ordered to reveal nothing. 'Let's say it's got t' do with the kid, Doc.'

'But I couldn't touch her without a heart pump, without . . .'

'I di'n' say you was gonna operate on the kid.' From the back seat, Audrey saw a reflection of the cold, colorless eyes in the rear-view mirror. 'Make like I di'n' say nothin', see?'

Something to do with Bonnie Castle, yet the instruments, the anesthetic, the surgeon, and the nurse were needed for another purpose. Why?

Marco added one more comment, after which he refused to communicate further. 'It's a tight squeeze, Doc. The boss is kinda shook up . . . know what I mean?'

'He didn't threaten me,' Dan said, more to himself than to others. 'He said I had to come, but he didn't sound like the tough operator I know.' Dan turned in the front seat to address Audrey. 'Don't be afraid, honey. Whatever Roger wants from us, he must need it in a big way. When I talked to him on the phone, I think the guy was crying.'

*   *   *

Marco stopped the Cadillac in the parking area behind the low-slung, modern stucco building which housed Dan Agnew's suite. 'Anybody in there?' he asked Dan.

'You mean in my office? No. My receptionist doesn't come in today. I don't keep regular office hours on Saturday . . . only by appointment.'

'What about some other doctor?'

'You'll see Dr. Voss' name on the door, but he's gone.'

'O.K.' Marco opened his door and slid out of the seat. 'Let's go.'

Dan followed suit.

'You stay here,' Marco told the hood in the

back seat. 'Keep the redhead company.' He slammed the car door and walked around to Dan's side of the car. 'Don't try bein' a hero. If we meet somebody you know, I'm a patient an' you're in a hurry. You got me?'

'No, you've got me,' Dan said. He glanced at Audrey over his shoulder. 'Be a good girl.'

'Be a *smart* one,' Marco said. He started toward the back entrance of the building with Dan at his side. Anyone observing them wouldn't have given Dan and his escort a second glance; Marco obviously wasn't forcing the doctor to accompany him, and there was no indication that pasty-face carried a gun. Dan could have made a break. Inside the office, he would have an even better opportunity.

But he won't, Audrey knew. He'll do as he's told and he'll come back here, because he knows what might happen if he doesn't.

The thought wasn't exactly comforting, yet her fear would be lessened by Dan's presence. Whatever was wanted of them, wherever they were going, it would be less frightening with Dan present. Still, it was a selfish thought, and Audrey wished she had the courage and selflessness to want Dan free . . . to face whatever lay ahead alone. Ashamed of her weakness, she waited for him to return, wondering how anyone could be ignorant enough to expect a surgeon to assemble instruments in an office for an unknown operation!

There was no sound in the car except the wheezy breath of the man beside her. He sat unbelievably still, his fabric-shielded gun pressed against her ribs. Lightly. Only enough pressure to make certain Audrey didn't forget it was there.

It seemed that a long time had elasped, though there was no way of gauging the time. When the suspenseful silence became unbearable, Audrey said, 'They should be coming back soon.'

Al's facial muscles seemed to be frozen. Neither hostile nor affable, as matter-of-factly as if they were waiting for a late dinner companion, he grunted, 'Yeah.'

After a while he began to whistle some tuneless melody between his teeth. When Marco and Dan emerged from the building, Dan carrying a black, professional bag, the man stopped whistling. Less than a minute later they were on their way.

Chapter 10

Audrey had never seen the Castle residence by daylight. In the morning sunshine, the house appeared even larger and more ostentatious than when she had first viewed it.

Years ago, she thought as the Cadillac

crunched up the long driveway. It must have been years ago when all this began. How many eons back had life been pleasant and promising, with no insane threat hanging over her head . . . when people like Roger Castle and Al and Marco were only characters in some of those impossibly violent TV shows that immortalized the roaring twenties?

As they neared the house, another car spurted from a parkway in front of the massive garage, following the circular drive in an opposite direction, with perhaps twenty-five yards of velvety grass separating it from the Cadillac, but only for a moment. Then it was gone, racing toward the opened exit gates.

It wasn't until Marco muttered, 'So long, fuzz,' that it registered in Audrey's mind; the small black-and-white sedan had been a police car!

'Roger's had visitors,' Dan remarked testily.

'Yeah,' Marco said. 'They been in an' out. Gettin' nowhere fast.'

'They haven't traced Eddy Cado?'

For a reply, Marco turned from the wheel to give Dan a long look of disgust. He stopped the car near the wide entrance stairway to the house, and from that time until they had entered the wide vestibule, neither Marco nor Al made any comment.

Vince—apparently Roger's most trusted confidant—was waiting for them. 'You guys get lost,' he told the others. Addressing Dan

135

and Audrey, he said, 'Roger's upstairs in his room.'

No words wasted, and a gloom-filled, hush-voiced atmosphere! Marco and Al, having performed their assignment, disappeared. And then Dan and Audrey were following the big gorilla up a curved, thickly carpeted stairway and down a candelabra-lighted hall lined with what might have been valuable Flemish paintings; but Audrey's nervous system wasn't geared for art appreciation.

Vince stopped at a handsomely paneled door and turned the knob quietly. His quiet manner suggested that of a nurse rather than a bodyguard . . . or hired killer. 'Don't bug 'im,' he whispered hoarsely. 'He's in a bad way.'

'If he's sick enough for surgery, why doesn't? . . .'

Dan's sentence went unfinished. They were inside the opulently furnished bedroom, Vince closing the door behind them and discreetly turning the lock.

Audrey had been prepared for a demanding, belligerent Roger Castle, the boss wanting a shady job done and not above using force to get his way. Her first sight of him left her stunned.

Roger was pacing the floor as they came into the room, a wine-colored dressing gown hanging limply from his shoulders, his face swollen and puffy. Like the others, he had been awake all night, but the redness of his eyes indicated tears rather than sleeplessness. His head jerked upward as he became aware of visitors, and Audrey wondered when she had seen a more anguished expression.

'Doc . . . my God, I didn' think you'd ever get here!' As Roger crossed the room, his hands raked the sides of his face in an agitated gesture. 'Listen, I hated to use the strong-arm stuff, but I had no choice.' Roger ignored Audrey, addressing himself to Dan. 'I had t' be sure you got here, see? An' didn' tell nobody.' His voice cracked, and he slumped into a chair, his body trembling uncontrollably.

Dan and Audrey found chairs opposite him. Vince posted himself near the door, as though he were standing guard.

'You might tell us what's coming off,' Dan said irritably. 'If someone needs medical attention, I don't have to be summoned at gunpoint. Frankly, I don't . . .'

'They . . . gone?' Roger's broken question was meant for Vince.

'Yeah.'

'The cops,' Roger explained. 'Jeez, we get rid of one batch, there's another one.'

'Are they making any headway?' Dan asked.

'If they get to Eddie Cado first'—Roger shuddered and covered his face with his hands—'he'll think I sicked 'em on him. *He'll kill her!*' His hand dropped to his lap, clenching in tense white fists, and his eyes seemed to be imploring Dan for some miraculous answer to an unrevealed problem.

'Her?'

'Bonnie! He's got Bonnie!'

Audrey caught a gasping breath. 'How could he? . . .'

'He's a maniac! Eddie gets off his junk, he's crazy.' Roger stood up and started walking from his chair to the window and back again in quick, agitated steps. 'He didn't go far when he ran outta here last night. After we left to take Jeff to the hospital . . . he must've come back.' Enormous tears coursed across the suntanned face now. 'I got back from the hospital, her nurse was still asleep. But my kid was gone!'

'I should've stayed here,' Vince mumbled from his post near the door. Audrey had forgotten he was in the room.

'You know how sick she is!' Roger was leaning over Dan, gripping his shoulder, his voice that of a grief-crazed man. 'If she gets scared . . . if he don't treat her right . . . and he's mean, Doc. He's crazy mean, an' he hates me!'

Dan was on his feet. 'And you haven't reported this? A kidnaping?'

Roger's eyes protruded from his face, his jaw rigid in the paralysis of terror. He was apparently too choked up to speak above a raspy whisper. 'I can't! Doc, I can't! You don't know Eddie. He'll kill my kid!'

Dan exchanged brief, puzzled glances with Audrey. 'Did he leave a ransom note? What does he want?'

'He wants . . .' For a moment it appeared as though Roger would collapse from a stroke. Then, managing to compose himself, he cried, 'He wants money. He wants junk.'

'I can't help him there, Roger.'

'I know. So I know that! That's the least I got t' deliver.' Roger was back at the window again, staring wildeyed into the formal garden below. Suddenly he whirled around, hysteria raising his voice to a strident pitch. 'You gotta do this fer me, Doc! You do it, I'll see you never have t' work another day in your life.' He jabbed a shaking index finger in Audrey's direction. 'Her neither. You gotta do this, 'cause if I don't never see Bon again, you two . . . you're gonna get carried outta here feet first!'

Dan's calm was impressive. He spoke to the frightened hood the way he might have addressed a worried patient. 'What is it you want me to do, Roger?'

Roger was back in his chair, shaking his head from side to side in tortured disbelief. His forehead glistened with perspiration, and Audrey guessed that unless his frustration was relieved in at least some minor fashion, the man would explode.

'What do you want from us?' Dan repeated.

139

Roger closed his eyes. There was a deadly silence, and then the words spilled out of him breathlessly. 'I told you Eddie's crazy. He's hung up on junk, but he's got a thing about lookin' out fer this weirdo of a brother he's got. Monk. You ever see pictures o' Monk? Like in the paper, when the two of 'em made the break?'

Dan admitted he hadn't, and Audrey said, 'I don't remember.'

'He's in the next room,' Roger said tonelessly.

'He's in . . .'

'In the next room!' Roger whispered hoarsely. 'Eddie's idiot brother!'

'If Eddie Cado's really that concerned about his brother,' Audrey said, 'you . . . don't have anything to worry about, do you? How did you manage to get hold of him?'

Roger shook his head again, disgusted. 'I didn't, I didn't! You think Eddie's a jerk? Kooky in the head, sure. But smart. Smart! He sent Monk here. Kidnaps my kid—every cop in the country lookin' fer both of 'em, an' he sends Monk here! You wanna know why?' Roger was out of his chair again, heading toward the door. 'You come an' see his face! A guy can't hide out with a face like Monk got.'

Roger stopped at the door, turning toward Dan. 'He knows I've got connections. Eddie, he knows I got all kindsa friends . . . like doctors.'

'People you own?' Dan spoke in a level monotone.

'Don't give me that!' Roger was shrilling the words now. If she could have put the brutal assault upon Jeff Beaumont out of her mind, Audrey would have felt a genuine pity for the man. At the moment, she could only consider the tiny girl whose dark hair snarled over her head exactly like Roger Castle's. If the child was still alive, nothing her distraught father asked of them could be too much. Not if it meant Bonnie's life.

Roger was speaking, almost screaming now, his vocal chords sore and constrained. 'Listen, Doc. This guy needs a plastic-surgery job. Fix 'im up so he won't be recognized on the street. See . . . see, Eddie knows he'll get caught,— they both will. Monk's face bein' one nobody could ferget. But he's nuts, see? Eddie . . . he wouldn' ditch Monk. Not him. So he knows I can get Monk fixed up. I hand over the dough an' I'—Roger paused, his face turning red.— 'I'll see can I get him his junk. Must be someplace!'

'We'll find someplace,' Vince said reassuringly.

'Then . . . the way I got it from this moron—from this Monk—he goes back t' Eddie with a new mug the cops don't recognize. And when I deliver Monk, I get my kid!'

141

'Roger, it's out of the question.'

'*No, it ain't!* It's what I gotta do! You've gotta help me, Doc!'

'But don't you understand? Plastic surgery's an art. It takes weeks of prior preparation.' Dan was arguing persuasively, but Audrey noticed that the target of his argument wasn't listening. Roger was too close to nervous collapse to listen to reason.

'I don't have weeks, Doc! I want my kid back while she's still alive!'

'I know, we all do.' Dan walked toward the door. 'Look, you don't understand what a facial reconstruction involves. You need a specialist. And you need time to design the finished result, you need time to take grafts and time for them to take hold.'

'I don't have time!' Roger screamed. 'Eddie wants results. Monk said . . . I get the kid back when Eddie sees results.'

'Roger, think!' Dan pleaded. 'Assuming I was prepared for plastic surgery, assuming the results were good—and mind you, that's assuming miracles—it would take at least two weeks before you could demonstrate the results to this . . . Monk's brother.'

'I told you I don't! . . .'

'*We* don't have two weeks! I'm Bonnie's doctor. Do you think I don't know what shock and fear and improper pare are going to do to her? Roger, be sensible! Every hour we wait brings her that much closer to death. Call the police!'

'He'll kill her! He said . . . he told Monk to tell me . . . if the cops are called, she gets it right there. You don't know Eddie Cado!'

Audrey had joined Dan near the door. He looked to her, momentarily, for support, and Audrey heard herself saying, 'What are you going to do . . . wait two weeks and trade a botched-up surgical job for a child's body?'

Roger's arm shot out, his palm slamming hard against Audrey's face. She felt the stinging blow reverberating at the base of her brain and cried out, staggering backward. In the next second Dan had lunged furiously at Roger Castle, and the reprisal was met in almost the same instant by Vince.

Audrey was uncertain whether the fist jabbed at Dan's midriff came before or after the gun Vince whipped from under his jacket. She heard the echo of her own scream, saw Dan double up after the thudding impact of a vicious blow. And then Roger was shouting like a hysterical fishwife, 'You want the redhead to stay alive? You wanna see what Vince can do once I give the word? You gonna operate on the Monk? Or you gonna tangle with me, if somethin' happens to Bonnie?'

Maniacal screams, added to the leveled gun, eliminated the possibility of reason! Audrey put her arm around Dan's shoulders, bolstering him, and Vince's ugly face contorted to form an auxiliary command:

143

'Monk's in here.'

Vince's gun didn't waver as he unlocked and opened the door. If there was an uncertainty, it was in Roger Castle's approach; apparently unsatisfied with the honest emotional appeal and the explosion of violence, he was apologizing as Dan and Audrey left the room: 'We been good friends, Doc! I'm goin' outta my head! You gotta do this fer me! Anything you want . . . the rest of your life, you name it, it's yours, but you gotta do this! *I gotta see Bonnie again!*'

Audrey didn't turn back to see him, but the sobbing quality of Roger's final outburst was enough to convince her that he couldn't be held responsible for whatever happened. In a world where everything belonged to him, Roger Castle had lost the one thing that mattered. Whether he cried, pleaded, threatened, struck out, or killed, he had to have his child back.

'I'm going to try,' Dan said tersely. 'Not for you. Because of what Audrey means to me. Keep that in mind, Roger.'

Vince was prodding them down the hall.

'I can't help myself, Doc.' Roger was a contrite, whining spectacle now. 'Listen, the spot I'm in . . . the way Eddie thinks . . . I gotta deal with 'im. I gotta stay ten miles from the smell of a cop . . . keep 'em from comin' upstairs, maybe askin' where's the kid . . .'

'They must have seen the shape you're in,'

Dan observed.

'They think I'm all shook about Jeff.'

'I imagine you are,' Audrey said.

'Yeah, but this thing! I'm goin' out of my head! I got one hope. Give Eddie what he wants.'

'In two weeks, Roger? When the mess I make of this guy's face heals?' Dan had recovered enough from the sudden blow to come back with a furious argument. 'I can't do what you want or what the Cados want! It can't be done! And while you're wasting time with the impossible, the police could be combing the city. There'd be a chance!'

Roger was less certain of himself now, his assault weaker. 'I'm her old man . . . I ought to . . .'

'I'm her doctor,' Dan said firmly, 'and I'm telling you she won't survive two weeks without professional care. Don't you realize the police are looking for Cado anyway? He's an escaped convict. And didn't you tell them he stabbed Jeff? So you can't keep the police away from him, but you can let them know there's a kidnaping involved. Use your head!'

'They spot him, they shoot Cado. No questions.' Vince seemed to be growing impatient with the trend of the conversation. 'You gonna let every news program start blabbin' he's got the kid? You know what Eddie's gonna do, boss.' Vince glared his contempt at Dan. 'This creep don't know

Eddie!'

'Shut up, Vince!' Roger pounded his fist, against his forehead, as though he might be trying to force a decision from his tortured mind.

'You're taking a hopeless gamble,' Audrey said. 'Dan isn't lying to you. He can't do plastic surgery under these ...'

'Shut up! You, too!' Roger broke in suddenly, his voice erupting from his throat in a wild, high-pitched cry. 'Don't anybody try an' mix me up! *No more!* We do it the way I said it's gonna be done!'

'That's all I was sayin'',' Vince growled.

A few seconds later he ushered Dan and Audrey into the adjoining bedroom. Evidently Roger wanted no part of the scene, and Vince relayed his instructions. 'Make the guy look good, Doc. There ain't no phone in here. An' I'll be outside the door, so play it cool.' He favored Audrey with a sadistic half-smile. 'Heroes got a way a gettin' hurt aroun' here.'

Audrey had expected the thug to remain in the room with them. Perhaps he had orders from Roger, or perhaps he was squeamish when someone else was handling the knife. Whatever the reason, Vince closed the door behind himself without further discussion. Exactly two seconds later, the door to the adjoining bathroom opened, and a squat, hunched figure stepped into the room.

Audrey's gasp was involuntary; the man

146

didn't need to be reminded of his looks by a shocked reaction. For he had risked his life to come here, and his doting brother was gambling a death sentence for kidnaping against an insane hope that unplanned surgery would erase one of nature's cruelest errors.

An uncontrollable shudder ran through Audrey's body. He was staring at them now, motionless, the bulging eyes glowing with resentment. *How handsome and hateful we must look to him,* Audrey thought. Yet the heartlessness of threatening an ailing child's life in exchange for a face that would not elicit gasps hardened her against pity.

He didn't have the right. But, God knew, Monk Cado had the need!

Chapter 11

Monk Cado was sitting on the edge of the bed, speaking to them in a thin, nasal voice completely devoid of inflection. 'Eddy said not to let nobody knock me out.'

Dan had just gone through the motions of examining his 'patient's' face. It had been a depressing sight, watching the blend of suppressed rage and pathetic eagerness with which Monk submitted to the inspection. Under a plastic surgeon's hand, years ago, there would have been an excellent chance that a miraculous improvement in the twisted features would have created a second miracle and changed a warped personality. Now, even if the bulging forehead and protruding upper lip were reconstructed, the misshapen nose rebuilt, and the almost nonexistent chin given a new contour, Monk would probably continue to carry the scars of his simian face inside himself. He was ugly. They didn't call him 'Monk' without reason. And a tiny mind combined with a tortured soul to form only one solution: hate the ones who had been lucky!

Yet even if a wonderful change could be wrought by plastic surgery, there was no possibility that it would be done here and now, under impossibly crude conditions. Dan had tried to explain that to Roger. Perhaps, in a rational state of mind, Roger would have been made to understand that plastic surgery was a highly specialized field, far outside the area in which a cardiac surgeon could have any real competence. Time, knowledge, hospital conditions . . . Roger Castle might have been made to understand their importance in spite of his ignorance of medical procedure—*if* he had been in his right mind. But now, Roger was far from being able to think clearly, and the moronic character with the unbelievably distorted features seemed to know even less. His bright big brother had sent him here for an operation that would make him more attractive . . . and less conspicuous. Worshipfully, Monk Cado was determined to follow Eddie's instructions to the letter. One of those orders he was repeating now:

'Eddie said, "Don't let this doctor give you no ether or nothin'."'

Whatever Dan had in mind, he was being exceedingly calm and reassuring. 'I'm not going to give you ether, Mr. Cado. But you realize that I can't perform surgery unless you're anesthetized . . . at least locally.'

'What's that?' Monk asked.

'I'll have to give you an injection to deaden your nerves. Otherwise you wouldn't be able to stand the pain, and I wouldn't be able to do my job.' Dan spoke in a soft, paternal tone. He might have been addressing an elderly coronary victim in his consulting room. 'You understand that, don't you? I'm going to do my best, but you'll have to cooperate.'

Monk nodded dumbly, but he was still hesitant. 'Eddie's smart. He says if you knock me out, I might say too much.'

'A lot of people believe that,' Dan said. And he was being perfectly honest. 'The truth is, people don't reveal anything under an anesthetic that they wouldn't ordinarily say. All I'm going to do, Mr. Cado'—he made it a point to address the miserable little hoodlum in respectful terms, divorcing himself from Roger's enemy camp and working to win Monk's confidence—'all I'm going to do is see that you don't feel any pain.' Steadily, getting his point across, he added, 'When I start cutting into your flesh—and I have to do that to make changes in your face—you won't feel a thing.'

The apelike forehead raveled in a bewildered frown, 'I allus do like Eddie says.'

Audrey decided to add her reassurance. In what she hoped was a lulling, confident tone, she said, 'Your brother wouldn't want you to suffer. You know that. The doctor wants you to take the bandages off in a week or so and see a brand-new face. And he doesn't want the operation to hurt.'

Monk was trembling now, confused by the unique position of having to make a decision and probably as fearful of his brother's censure as he was of the agony connected with having his features rearranged by sharp instruments.

Audrey was laying them out now: scalpels, scissors . . . the contents of Dan's armamentarium, sensing that the psychological effect would frighten Monk into submission. She had no idea what Dan was planning to do. Certainly he wasn't going to attempt a reconstruction under these circumstances. He had made no mention of taking grafts from other parts of Monk's body, made no provision for the sterilization of instruments. And heaven only knew he wasn't going to attempt the impossible. But he had asked

Audrey to lay out the instruments on the nightstand beside the bed, acting as though this was an operating room and the slightly dusty, carved mahogany table was a Mayo-stand!

While he pondered, Monk stole several furtive glances at the gleaming steel blades. To any layman, they would have looked awesome; they must have struck a chill of fear in the heart of this ignorant misfit.

'You won't feel a thing,' Dan was repeating soothingly.

Audrey continued to spread out the threatening and mysterious objects fashioned from surgical steel, working purposefully, seeing fear light up the close-set yellow-gray eyes of the 'patient.'

What was Dan going to do? He sounded so sincere, so believable, that for a moment Audrey wished that the hopes he was raising in Monk Cado had some basis in reality. Knowing better, she could only wonder, not how Dan would satisfy Monk, but how he would appease Eddie and, more pertinent, Roger Castle. Incredibly, Dan gave every indication that he would use those gleaming instruments. But what surgical nurse in possession of all her faculties could believe that he would?

'I'm going to have my nurse prepare an injection,' Dan said quietly, almost casually. 'I want you to trust me, Mr. Cado. I hope you

151

do, because it's important for both of us.'

The strangely chimplike head nodded slowly; Monk's eyes were pitifully trusting now.

'Fine. Miss West . . . if you'll prepare the hypodermic, please.'

Audrey searched through the hastily packed bag. 'With novocaine, Doctor?'

'No, I think we'll get better results with the sodium.'

Sodium? Audrey frowned. What sort of gibberish was this? Was Dan merely stalling for time? And if so, what did he expect her to do?

Perhaps because they had worked together silently so many times, communicating only with their eyes, Audrey looked up from her search.

Dan was staring at her meaningfully. 'I know it's there,' he said. 'I don't know how I happened to make the selection . . .' Now he seemed to be selecting his words carefully, aiming them at Audrey in an attempt to communicate with her without being understood by Monk Cado. 'Considering the unexpected prognosis, Miss West, the necessity for determining unknown factors relative to our cardiac patient's recovery . . . to determine *location* . . . I believe the choice of anesthesia was fortuitous.'

Audrey let the words sink into her consciousness—'. . . our cardiac patient's recovery.' Nothing to do with plastic surgery. 'Recovery!' Dan was talking about Bonnie Castle . . . about determining *her* location! Then why was Dan's choice of anesthesia 'fortuitous'?

She might have figured it out after a few minutes of evaluation. As it happened, in the process of unpacking the hurriedly assembled instrument bag, her hand fell upon a glass ampule.

Dan was observing her closely now; Monk seemed to be detached from the proceedings, and apparently Dan's message had gone over his head. Audrey read the label.

She didn't repeat aloud what she read. Monk might be stupid, but drugs had been his livelihood, and it wasn't safe to assume that he had never heard of sodium amytal. He might even know, as Audrey remembered the instant her fingers closed over the ampule, that it was popularly known as 'the truth drug.'

Audrey looked deeply into Dan's eyes, now, letting him know she understood. There wasn't going to be an operation. There was going to be an interview that might spell the difference between life and death for an innocent child.

'Do you want me to prepare the hypo, Doctor?' Audrey asked.

'Please. We want Mr. Cado to be as comfortable as possible.'

'This stuff . . . you ain't gonna knock me

out?' There was only a hint of suspicion in Monk's voice now.

'We're only going to make the operation possible,' Dan said.

Carefully, Audrey broke open the ampule, mixing the powder inside it with the contents of another bottle she had located inside the bag—ten c.c.'s of sterile water. When the sodium amytal had dissolved, she filled a hypodermic needle with the mixture.

Why hadn't Roger Castle thought of this? As quick as he was to use force, why hadn't he thought of a means to make Monk reveal his brother's whereabouts, and along with that information, find his child? He was too terrified, she concluded. Roger was too familiar with the consequences of the double-cross in his world of violence to do anything but follow Eddie Cado's instructions to the letter. He would be furious if he knew what Dan had in mind. And if Dan's idea failed, Roger would be more than furious. He would be ready to kill again.

Dan was in the bathroom, going through the crude motions of 'scrubbing.' Was he actually going to attempt some semblance of an operation? Audrey wondered. Whatever his plan, she was committed to assist him. And after the long, lonely months of being critical of his course, it was ironic that this surge of pride in his intelligence and skill should sweep over her under these unorthodox and tense circumstances. There was no way of knowing what would happen, and the possibility of brutal, sudden death for both of them could hardly be discounted. Audrey turned her mind away from what might follow. This moment, *now*, she was of value to Dan Agnew in a crucial experiment. She had never respected him more, loved him more, or felt that he needed her more.

Monk was saying something to her. 'Hey . . . you a real nurse?'

'Yes, I am. I work at the Hollywood Memorial Hospital.'

The distorted face stretched into an approving grimace that was intended to be a smile. 'How 'bout him? He a real doctor?'

'He's one of the best surgeons in the area,' Audrey said solemnly.

Monk pondered that fact for a few moments in his miniscule brain. Then, with a confidence that betrayed his limited reasoning capacities, he said, 'Eddie was right. He said, "Don't worry . . . Roger's gonna get you the best doctor he could find." '

'Eddie's always right, isn't he?' Audrey said.

Monk nodded. 'Yeah, he's smart. Nobody's smart as Eddie.'

Dan had returned to the bedroom, amazingly cheerful and displaying an exemplary bedside manner. 'Well, now! We have important work to do. Right, Mr. Cado?'

Monk lifted a hand to his frighteningly

155

inhuman face, running his fingers over the features and wincing in disgust. In a sense, it was a farewell gesture. Poor, miserable specimen . . . he really believed that when he looked at that face again it would be unrecognizably changed . . . and it could only be changed for the better. In spite of the rottenness of his life, (a rottenness that had its foundations in ignorance and physical rejection), Monk was still a human being whose dream differed sharply from the horrible reality he saw each morning in his mirror. Audrey wished that the 'operation' for which Dan was preparing could result in renewed hope instead of a crushing disappointment that could only feed Monk Cado's hatred of other men.

Monk was wearing a wrinkled, printed rayon sport shirt of an undetermined pattern and color. When Dan asked him to lie down on the quilted satin-covered bed, Monk obeyed, childlike, and obligingly rolled up his shirt sleeve.

There were needle marks on Monk's arm; it was a scarred but healed pincushion of evidence. Audrey read the old punctures to mean that Monk had once carried a heavy habit, that he had probably gone through a torturous 'cold-turkey' cure in prison, and that he had either resisted the temptation or found drugs unavailable since his escape.

Audrey swabbed an area above the abused

vein with alcohol. With the hypo needle poised above Monk's arm, she looked to Dan for direction.

'Two c.c.'s,' Dan ordered.

Monk drew a loud, strong inhalation, closing his eyes as Audrey plunged the needle into his vein and released the measured amount of sodium amytal.

An unnatural silence fell over the room while they waited for the drug to take effect. Audrey filled the time by rearranging the unsterilized instruments. Dan searched his pockets, coming forth with an address book and a black plastic ball-point pen.

'Record the patient's reactions,' Dan whispered. Audrey took the little book and the pen from him.

It may only have been a few minutes, though it seemed like a lifetime, before Monk's eyes reflected an uncontrollable drowsiness. When the eyelids had closed and Monk's muscles showed signs of complete relaxation, Dan left the bedside and walked to the door, listening carefully.

He returned to whisper in Audrey's ear, 'I'll have to keep it quiet; Vince is out there, all right. Write down everything Cado says.'

Audrey heard the erratic thumping of her heart reverberating against her eardrums. Pen in hand, she waited for Dan's first question.

When it seemed safe to begin, Dan asked an innocuous, exploratory question:

157

'Is your name Monk Cado?'

'Frank Cado,' Monk replied. His voice had a zombilike, monotonous quality. 'Frank.'

'Where's your brother?' Dan persisted. 'Where is your brother staying?'

'Staying?'

'Yes, his address. Where is Eddie staying?' Dan was attempting to balance his volume; quiet enough to escape detection by the guard outside the door, yet firm and clear enough to penetrate the anesthetic fog enshrouding the man sprawled on the bed. 'What's the address, Frank?'

'Two thirty-one, Pacific Court.'

'In Los Angeles?'

There was a breathless pause. 'Long Beach.' Monk's groggy reply was repeated. 'Long Beach.'

'Is Eddie there alone?' Dan asked. Audrey scribbled the address onto a blank sheet in Dan's address book. 'Is someone else there with Eddie?'

'Girl. Little girl.'

'Bonnie Castle?'

Monk was silent, his head shaking from side to side as if to ward off the persistent questions.

'If he starts to come out of it, give him another couple of c.c.'s,' Dan whispered. 'I don't want him asleep, but I don't want him conscious, either.'

Audrey nodded. At the moment, Monk

158

Cado's condition presented no problem. Their only fear was that Dan's voice would carry outside to Roger Castle's henchman.

'Frank, tell me about the place where Eddie's staying.' Dan was speaking clearly, but his awareness of the need for secrecy had reduced his volume. Monk didn't respond, and he was forced to repeat himself. 'Tell me about the place, Frank. Is it an apartment?'

'Yeah. Apartment.'

'Is it on the first floor?'

'First floor,' Monk echoed. 'Up front.'

Dan went on to ask specific questions about the layout, checking occasionally to see that Audrey was recording every detail. 'When you were there, did he have the little girl with him?'

Monk shook his head again, and then he attempted to sit up, reacting strongly to the questioning.

Dan's raised eyebrows were a sufficient signal. Audrey set down the pen and address book, picking up the hypo needle once more. In his half-conscious state, Monk moaned as she injected a second dose of the sodium amytal into his vein.

Dan waited until their patient relaxed once more into the lethargic state, then repeated his question:

'Where was the little girl?'

'Back room. Room in the back.'

'Was she all right, Frank?'

'Cryin'. She was . . . cryin'.'

'Eddie sleeps in a room toward the front of the apartment?'

'Front room. Eddie sleeps on the couch.'

Monk's droning voice rose in volume. Audrey found herself watching the door, expecting a sudden interruption. Why was Dan asking these seemingly irrelevant questions, delaying the 'operation' and risking their lives by probing every minute detail?

Dan's semiwhispered questioning continued. By the time Audrey had finished filling most of the blank pages in the small leather book, she had recorded a virtual floor plan of the apartment in Long Beach. Now she began to understand why Dan had been so thorough. What escaped her now was his plan for the remainder of the 'operating-room' session.

Dan waited until she had returned his address book. Tucking it into his jacket pocket, he said, 'You'd better use his other arm this time, Audrey.'

'His other arm?'

'To shoot the remaining six c.c.'s. Not that he hasn't used both arms for a pincushion himself.'

Audrey circled the bed, carrying a small bottle of alcohol and cotton swab. When she had prepared Monk's left arm, Dan reversed the usual O.R. procedure and handed the hypodermic needle to her. 'I wanted him groggy for the questioning,' he said. 'Now let's get him to sleep.'

Audrey's eyes traveled the distance between Monk's face and the surgical instruments she had laid out on the bedside table. 'Dan, you . . .' She hesitated, reluctant to criticize him and acutely aware that whatever she said might be heard outside the room. As she returned the needle to the makeshift instrument stand next to Dan, she whispered, 'What are you going to do?'

Dan's loud, projected tone startled her. 'We can begin surgery now, Miss West.' He nodded his head toward the door, though she would have understood without the accompanying gesture that he was talking for someone else's benefit.

Audrey matched his tone, 'I'm ready, Doctor.'

He leaned to whisper in her ear. 'Look . . . I'm going to draw enough blood to leave a few stains on the bedspread. I'll splatter a few swabs and bandages to leave in the waste-basket. You with me?'

'Yes, but what about the? . . .'

'We'll use novocaine in case Monk wakes up before we're out of here. He'll feel a swollen, deadened effect . . . at least he won't give us away.'

'You think Roger's going to let us go?'

Dan broke the hushed dialogue with a sharp order: 'Scalpel!' He listened for a moment, but there was no sound outside the door, and he resumed the *sotto voce* instructions. 'There should be enough two-inch rollers in my bag to do a shawl bandage. With his entire head covered . . .'

Audrey raised crossed fingers. 'Just so no one asks for a premature unveiling.' It had been amazing, and fortunate, that Roger hadn't insisted that the operation be observed. In his confused state, they could only hope he would continue to be untypically careless.

Dan continued to bark meaningless orders, meanwhile faking the aftereffects of surgery. They worked slowly; not even the most ignorant layman would believe that Monk's features could be made presentable in less than two hours. Yet to stall too long without covering Monk's face would invite trouble. If Roger Castle or Vince chose to come into the room now, Dan would be forced to perform some semblance of an operation, or admit that he had been perpetrating a hoax.

When Audrey had completed the bandage, swathing Monk's head in thicknesses of white gauze, Dan sat down to write out 'feeding instructions,' prescribing a liquid, straw-fed diet 'until the pain subsides.'

After that there was no way to prolong the act without chancing that Monk would regain consciousness. He was moaning intermittently now, as if he were actually suffering. If they delayed too long, he would be awake. The novocaine numbness would wear off quickly, and when he felt no discomfort at all, he would expose them.

'Can't you keep him under for a longer period?' Audrey asked softly.

'Nothing left in that kit except morphine.'

'Wouldn't that? . . .'

'I've got to draw the line somewhere,' Dan murmured. He was looking at Monk's needle-scarred arms, the veins covered now by neat white squares of taped-down gauze. 'Those were all old punctures, Audrey. I know what he went through to kick the habit . . . and the odds are that it isn't kicked out of his head. I'm not going to be the guy who turns him back on.'

They were packing the last items, almost ready to start for the door when Audrey looked toward the bed. Their camouflaged 'surgery' looked realistic; the effect of the bloodstains on the quilted satin cover wasn't too obvious.

'He's going to hate me.' Dan formed the words with his lips, barely making any sound.

'Too bad he won't remember that you called him "Frank." He's probably been "Monk" or "Monkeyface" all his life.'

'I called him Mr. Cado, too,' Dan said, 'but he's still going to hate me.'

Monk was deep in drugged sleep when they opened the door, then closed it quietly behind them.

Vince was dutifully at his post, a chair drawn up next to the door and an ashtray full of cigarette butts on the floor beside him. He was on his feet instantly. 'You all done?' He eyed Dan suspiciously, and Audrey held her breath. He had been listening. He must have heard!

But apparently the distrustful attitude was standard operating procedure in the Castle ranks. Vince led them toward Roger's room as soon as Dan had replied, 'Finished. And I could use a drink.' He wore the look of a surgeon exhausted by an operating-room ordeal, and the request for a drink would be interpreted in the same way by the big hood.

Roger greeted them with a barrage of anxious questions. Had it gone all right? Would the Cado boys be satisfied? The guy wasn't in bad shape, was he? Jeez, they didn't even have boiling water . . . why didn't they ask for it? Couldn't a guy get some kind of infection if they didn't boil the instruments? Not that the dirty scum didn't deserve to kick off, but Eddie . . . if they crossed Eddie . . .

The strain of waiting had added measurably to Roger's nervousness. He looked genuinely sick from anxiety, and Audrey guessed he was near collapse.

'It's all fine,' Dan lied. 'Went off better than we expected under the crude conditions. That was a large order, Roger.'

'Yeah . . . I know, I know.' Roger was torn

between gratitude and confusion; it became certain that he hadn't figured out what to do next.

'The doc says he needs a drink,' Vince told him.

'He don't need no drink,' Roger barked. 'If the cops come aroun', he's here takin' care of Bonnie, see? Nobody comes upstairs. He tells 'em she can't be disturbed.'

Roger's voice cracked at the mention of his daughter's name, and Dan was quick to take advantage of the emotional turmoil. 'Rog, you're in a bad way. I'm going to prescribe a sedative for you. If you don't get some rest, you'll crack wide open.'

'You think I could sleep? Listen—listen, Cado said he'd *call* me.'

'And you'd better be in condition to think straight when he does,' Dan said. 'Before I go . . .'

'Who said you're goin' somewheres?' Vince asked.

If Dan wavered or showed fear, they wouldn't stand a chance. 'I happen to have an operation scheduled,' he said. Calmly. As though any fool would know better than to reason otherwise. 'Miss West goes on duty this evening. If either of us are delayed, or if we don't get some sleep before then, it won't look too good, will it?'

Roger glared at Vince, but he was still undecided. 'So you don't show up. That don't

165

mean they'll come here lookin'.'

'I think they will,' Dan said easily. 'To begin with, the police want to question me about Jeff.'

Vince coughed nervously and reached for a cigarette.

'And then, of course, those two cops saw us as we pulled in.'

Roger ran his hands over his hair and sank to a corner of the bed. 'So I let you go, you hightail it to the cops, report me for bringin' you here by force, tell 'em Bonnie's gone. You know what'll happen to her?'

'Roger, listen to me.' Dan moved closer to the bed, speaking as gently as he had spoken to win Monk Cado's confidence. 'I know the pressure you're under. You had to get someone for that operation. Do you think I'm going to hold it against you?'

'If it was my little girl,' Audrey said, 'I'd have done the same thing.'

Roger looked up at her with tormented eyes. 'You were sayin' a little while ago to call the cops.'

'We don't want them called now,' Dan pointed out. He added the inspired implication that he and Audrey were now outside the law themselves. 'Performing nonemergency surgery without a licensed anesthetist . . .'

'They wouldn't be in no trouble,' Vince insisted. 'They could say we made 'em do it.'

'Will you stop acting like I'm your worst enemy, Roger?' Dan aimed his efforts at the weakening member of the pair, the one who made the decisions. 'I'm glad we were able to help you out. Now I'm not going to ruin everything by running to the police. You were probably right . . . you know this Cado character. You know the best way to handle him.'

Audrey decided to attempt one last emotional appeal. 'Dr. Agnew and I love that little girl. We fought to bring her through that first operation. We want you to get her back safely because we're going to fight for her again!'

Roger was silent for a few seconds. Then, wearily, he said, 'Get Marco to drive 'em home.'

'Boss, you let 'em outta here, an' they . . .'

'Get Marco an' shut your damn mouth!' Vince started to protest, but Roger was on his feet, swaying, but furious now. 'We got enough trouble keepin' Bonnie's nurse out of the way, an' she lives here. What am I gonna do, run a hotel? Have fifteen people playin' peek-a-boo in the closets every time somebody comes nosin' around? You heard Doc. He fixed up Monk. He wouldn't . . . cross me.' Roger tried to take a step forward, but he lost his balance and fell back to the bed. 'Why don't he call?' He had forgotten about Dan and Audrey, holding his head in his hands and crying. 'Why

167

don't that hophead call?'

Vince left the room without saying any more.

'He'll call,' Dan said. 'And you won't have to wait two full weeks before you show him the results of my operation. Just don't let anyone disturb the bandages for . . . a week. If you want us to, Miss West and I will come and check on Monk's progress. She'll . . . have to redress the wounds.'

Dan had provided the clinching proof Roger needed; if 'Doc' and his nurse were offering to return, he could trust them not to involve the police, couldn't he?

'O.K.,' Roger said rapidly. 'O.K . . . thanks.' His eyes were closed, fiercely pressed shut, as if to blot out his misery.

Dan was scribbling something on his pad. When he had finished, he tore off the top sheet and set it down on a chest at the foot of the bed. 'Get someone to have this prescription filled for you. Get your nerves in order, Roger. I left instructions for Monk's care in his room.'

Roger wasn't listening. Roger's ears were tuned only to one sound—the ringing of a telephone bell, a call that would tell him Bonnie was still alive . . . that Eddie Cado was ready to fulfill his end of the bargain.

Neither Roger nor Vince had bothered to look into the room where Eddie's bandaged but untouched brother groaned in a deep sodium amytal sleep!

As he chauffeured them back to Audrey's apartment, Marco neither asked questions nor made any comments. Except when a newscaster on the Cadillac's radio announced that Jeff Beaumont's condition 'remained unchanged.'

'Is that good or bad?' Marco asked.

Dan made some sort of noncommital reply.

It's good, Audrey determined silently. It meant that Jeff was holding his own, and every hour improved his chances. It was only bad if you happened to be Roger Castle or a vicious punk named Vince.

Chapter 12

Irene Rafferty met Dan and Audrey at the door, a glass of papaya juice in her hand, an eyelet-embroidered Mexican blouse sloping from her bony shoulders, and an urgent message: 'Ye gods, where've you been, Audrey? The phone's been ringing like crazy.' She nodded curtly toward Dan. 'For him. I told them I hadn't seen him in ages.'

'The hospital.' Dan was on his way to the phone.

'And some gal with a low, come-hither delivery,' Irene added caustically. 'She wouldn't leave her name, but with that voice, she didn't have to.'

Dan was checking the inside page of the phone book.

'What's the matter?' Irene asked. She was headed for the sink with her empty glass. 'Is he so out of touch with the hospital that he has to look up the number?'

Audrey followed her to the kitchen. 'Irene, will you get the chip off your shoulder? Dan's calling the police. There's . . . been some trouble.'

'Before he checks on his patient?'

'He's concerned about another patient,' Audrey said. 'One who isn't getting the care Jeff's getting.'

Audrey's reluctance to disclose details and Dan's guarded telephone conversation melted Irene's icy disapproval. 'What's going on, for heaven's sake? I heard the news about Jeff Beaumont on TV . . . wasn't that horrible? Were you in the O.R. for that?' She wasn't willing to declare a truce with Dr. Agnew. 'You ought to be glad you weren't at that party with him!'

'Forget it, will you? Too much has happened. I can't tell you about it now. Just see that . . .' Audrey interrupted herself to cross over to the living-room window, peering outside for the third or fourth time to make certain that Marco and the Cadillac weren't in sight. 'Just see that the door is locked.'

'What did you do, rob a bank?'

'Irene . . . please!' Audrey was standing next to Dan at the secretary now, trying to understand what was being arranged even though she couldn't hear the other half of the conversation.

'. . . need an ambulance standing by, but not in sight of the apartment. I'll contact the hospital in Long Beach . . . Right. Just be sure the police there don't jump the gun before we arrive. Yes, practically a complete floor plan . . . No, we'll have to come with you. She's bound to need medical attention . . . Yes. And please see that no one gets to Beaumont. I've left orders at the hospital, but he needs real protection.'

Dan finished the call shortly afterward, hanging up exasperatedly and muttering, 'They've got to check and make sure I'm not some kind of nut. More delays . . .' He was dialing again, quickly, a familiar number this time, and then he was saying, 'Connect me with the fourth-floor nurses' station, please.'

Audrey waited until Dan had completed his call to Hollywood Memorial. When he dropped the receiver, he turned to her, excluding Irene by his hushed tone. 'Jeff's doing beautifully . . . well enough to make a statement. The head nurse says there's a small delegation waiting to get into his room right now.'

'What kind of delegation?'

'The law and the press. I've given orders to

keep reporters out.'

'Roger's going to find out soon enough that Jeff's going to live, isn't he?'

'He's going to find out any minute now that you report a kidnapping to the authorities . . . you don't negotiate with the kidnapper on your own, promising him money and drugs. You don't kidnap a doctor and nurse, or try forcing them to perform an impossible operation. He's going to find out all that before Jeff is through telling the police who stabbed him. And unless we were guessing wrong, that's the only count he won't be able to wriggle out of. Attempted murder.'

'Then what difference does it make if the reporters get to Jeff? You don't have to worry about Roger any more.'

'No. But we can't take the chance that one of those waiting reporters wasn't hired by the wrong syndicate. I mean by Roger. Don't you see, Audrey? He'll be forgiven everything else. He'll be the respectable businessman caught in a desperate situation. What man wouldn't break the law to save his child's life? But Roger's got his whole future riding on whether or not Jeff lives or dies, whether he talks or he doesn't. If you had this much at stake, if you had unlimited funds and no conscience, what would you do?'

'I'd . . . make sure Jeff Beaumont didn't live long enough to talk. But that wouldn't be easy.'

'I'm betting he's hired someone to try. If he didn't, it's because Bonnie's disappearance threw him. And in that case I'd bet someone else took care of it.'

'Vince?'

Dan nodded. 'I could be wrong, but I told the detective about that, too. We'll have to sign a complaint before they can pick up Roger on the kidnapping charge. But they'll find Monk Cado in his house. And they won't find Bonnie. That'll convince them my call wasn't a false alarm.'

'What about Bonnie?'

'I explained the situation. That was the Beverly Hills station I called . . . in fact, I talked to someone who's working on the Beaumont case.'

'Why didn't you call the L.A. department, Dan?'

'Bonnie was kidnapped from Beverly Hills. The police there practically never involve the public, but I've convinced them that barging in and shooting it up is as likely to be fatal to the kid as . . . having Eddie Cado discover he's been double-crossed. They're on their way over to pick us up.'

'Us?'

'The detectives need our floor plan to get to her. And if she's still alive, two familiar faces and proper care might . . .'

'You don't have to explain! I want to go, of course. I didn't think they'd let us.' Audrey's eyes filled with tears. 'Oh, Dan, that poor, sick baby. Do you remember how sweet she was? The way she managed to smile . . . when she had all she could do to get her breath? Did you tell them to hurry?'

'They'll hurry,' Dan assured her.

Audrey turned away from him, unable to control the tears. 'Maybe you'll have time to make your . . . other call. I'll go freshen up and leave you alone.'

'What other call?'

Audrey started to remind him that Ginger Lampton had apparently been trying to reach him. But the gentle touch of his hands on her shoulders told her he hadn't asked a question. Even when the words were repeated against her ear, fervent and intimate, she knew Dan wasn't asking her a question. He was telling her the calls held no meaning for him.

'Turn around, Audrey. Let me look at you.' The warm pressure of his fingers urged her to face him.

'I can't, Dan. I'm a . . mess. No sleep for . . .'

But he was looking into her eyes now, not searchingly, but as though he had long ago found what he was looking for and, having lost it, had miraculously found it once more. 'I've missed you, Audrey. I didn't have sense enough to know it at the time, but I missed you terribly. All this wasted time!'

'It wasn't wasted, Dan, if you learned that.'

He kissed her, holding her in a desperate grip that left Audrey gasping for air. When he released her, Dan said, 'It's like coming home. Honey, if I didn't know it before, I knew it when Roger threatened you. I knew it again when you started talking about that little girl and crying.' He cupped Audrey's face in his palms and planted a tender kiss on her forehead. 'I know it now, Audrey. For keeps. I love you.'

If Irene was still around, she was being discreetly silent. Audrey had forgotten about her, and certainly Dan had behaved as though they were alone. Remembering, Audrey disengaged herself from Dan's arms. But she was remembering more than decorum in the presence of a third party. There was someone else to remember. 'Dan, it's not enough to say, "what other call?". You're engaged to Ginger Lampton, aren't you?'

He colored. 'In a manner of speaking.'

'What does that mean? Are you or aren't you?'

Dan shook his head tiredly, like someone awakening from a bad dream. 'She expects me to marry her.'

'Does she love you? That's the important question.'

'I don't know.' Dan sighed. 'Among those people . . . it's hard to be sure of anything. Things happen so fast. Suddenly you pick up a newspaper and a gossip columnist has you engaged. You think back, and . . . somehow, in some foggy moment, you remember that you did ask someone to marry you, and that . . . at the time it seemed terribly important to you.' He looked toward Audrey, tiredness and confusion etching deep lines across his forehead. 'I only know I'm sick of running around in circles. Sicker yet of being forced to play detective in a league I don't understand. Audrey . . . I want to pick up where I left off. Where Dr. Voss left off.' He turned his eyes toward the carpet, shamefaced. 'Do you know I haven't written to him yet? I wouldn't have known what to say. I found myself . . . writing in a strange language, not the language he'd recognize or care about.'

'He'd like to hear that,' Audrey said quietly.

'I'll get back,' Dan promised. 'If he still believes in me, if *you* do, I'll . . .'

'You have to come back with no strings attached,' Audrey said. 'I love you, Dan. But it's not going to be any good if you start out by . . . hurting someone else the way I've been hurt.'

'I'll talk to Ginger. She's never really been serious about anything except her career. I know she'll change her mind about me.'

'Then she's told you she loves you.'

'Yes. Yes, but I know it's . . .'

'We won't talk about it now,' Audrey said firmly.

'Audrey, I've *got* to.'

'When you're free, Dan. 'When your conscience is clear. We'll talk about it then.'

They were surrounded by an oppressive silence after that, and Audrey wondered if she hadn't been unfair. He had come back to her; wasn't that what she had wanted? And did she have to grind the errors of the past into his conscience after he had admitted them? Forgive, accept, love that was all she had to do and the dream was realized! It would be so easy to do! And what was she asking from him? A written release from a woman who, according to Jeff Beaumont, collected male scalps the way other women collected perfumes or fine china.

We're too tired for decisions, Audrey decided. She walked to the kitchen to plug in the coffeepot and discovered that Irene wasn't there; Irene had probably made a polite exit to her room. *We're too exhausted to think clearly, and it's not over yet!*

She was about to pour the coffee when Dan called her name from the living room.

'Audrey, they're here.'

She joined him at the picture window, looking out to see a uniformed officer on a motorcycle at the curb. Parked behind him was an inconspicuous dark sedan. The men who approached the apartment were dressed in plain business suits.

There wasn't going to be time for coffee, and it was just as well. A little girl whose years

177

had been numbered without surgery was living on borrowed minutes now . . . *if* they were lucky and she were still alive.

Chapter 13

Less than three-quarters of an hour after the screaming sirens cut a swath through Saturday afternoon traffic in Hollywood, the four occupants of the detectives' car, preceded by the roaring motorcycle, pulled up to a spot on Highway 101 to keep a prearranged rendezvous with Long Beach police.

It had been a nightmarish ride, yet one that had raised Audrey's respect for the efficiency and the intricate communications systems employed by guardians of the law.

Racing toward their destination, the two detectives in the front seat had analyzed the information recorded by Audrey during Monk Cado's drugged sleep. It formed the basis for a plan in which Long Beach officers, alerted by the Beverly Hills station, would cooperate.

Most of the terse, methodical planning was as unintelligible to Audrey as operating-room terminology would have been to the plainclothesmen. She only knew that they were weighing the possibilities and preparing for any eventuality. And that their broad-daylight attempt to capture Eddie Cado would not be without risk to them personally. The probability that Eddie Cado would kill to resist capture was considered, but only in technical terms; the problem was to rescue Bonnie Castle without shocking her.

The highway meeting lasted no more than a minute or two.

'The place is surrounded now,' one of the detectives said as he returned to the car. 'No sign of life in the apartment. They're waiting for us.'

'Would . . . would he be less suspicious,' Audrey asked, 'if I came to the door? I could pretend I'm a saleswoman or . . .'

'Thanks, miss,' the detective next to the driver said. 'We appreciate your help, but I'm afraid you and Dr. Agnew will have to stay out of the way.'

Dan patted Audrey's hand. 'You've had quite a day, darling. S'pose you let the professionals take over?'

They remained silent for a long time after that, but Dan's hand remained closed over Audrey's, reassuring her with its warm contact. There was no way to lessen the rising fear of what lay ahead, but it was comforting to know that Dan was beside her. Nothing in the present or future would be unbearable with Dan at her side.

Almost two miles from where the impromptu conference had been held, the motorcycle policeman pulled to the side of the

Pacific Coast Highway, allowing their car to turn into a side street unaccompanied. They drove three blocks and then pulled up in front of a cluster of pink stucco courtyard apartments that had long passed their prime.

'We're half a block from the address,' the driver said. 'Please don't leave the car. We'll call you if you're needed.'

'Good luck,' Dan said.

Both men got out of the sedan, one of them walking down the block toward another group of dilapidated one-story apartments almost identical with those before which they had parked. His partner cut through the yard of a weatherbeaten frame bungalow situated between the two units of apartments. They might have been selling encyclopedias; certainly there was nothing about the car or the men who had climbed out of it to indicate police action.

There was a faint breeze blowing from the ocean. Audrey watched it ruffle the magenta blossoms of a massive bougainvillea that had climbed to cover part of the roof over the frame bungalow. Still, the air inside the car was hot and heavy, made weightier by Audrey's constricted breath. 'She's *got* to be all right, Dan.'

Dan said nothing, only nodding grimly.

'She's such a fragile little thing . . .' Audrey let her mind drift, remembering her preoperative visit with the child . . . the

Dresden-doll loveliness and amazingly unspoiled personality. It seemed impossible that Bonnie Castle was the daughter of a man who could order others to spare a life . . . or kill, depending upon his convenience. And worse, it seemed unjust that the physical handicaps imposed upon the child should be aggravated in this terrifying, brutal manner. 'She's got to be all right,' Audrey repeated.

It was a whispered prayer to which Dan responded by pressing her hand tightly. He was sitting forward in the car seat, his eyes straining against the afternoon sun, watching intently as one of the detectives approached the door of the first apartment in that colorless row just down the street.

They reported to each other in tense, breathless sentences. 'He's knocking at the door.'

'I don't see any of the others, do you?'

'That's good. Cado won't see them, either.'

'He doesn't answer.'

'Oh, Dan, suppose he isn't there?'

Gone away and taken the ailing child with him? Or left her here . . . because her lifeless body no longer had ransom value? Audrey edged forward in the seat. 'There doesn't seem to be any . . .'

'Audrey!'

Dan's electric whisper turned her eyes from the barely visible scene toward the figure at which Dan was gesturing.

'I wouldn't swear to it,' Dan muttered, 'but he just looks like the guy I saw running across Roger's lawn.'

The man was hurrying along the sidewalk at their right, a small brown paper bag in his arms. He was evidently coming from the small bait and grocery store they had passed just after turning off the highway. Head down, he paid no attention to the car as he went by, moving in jerky, nervous steps past the first group of apartments. As he reached the hedge-bordered walk in front of the wooden house, he lifted his head, looking toward the other apartments. He couldn't have helped seeing the plainclothesman at the door. Across the street, another of the detectives moved behind a bamboo fence; he would have been unseen by anyone inside the apartment, but from the other man's oblique angle, he must have appeared suspicious. The man on the walk came to a full stop, as though he had applied mechanical brakes. In almost the same second, he did an about-face and started to retrace his steps, attempting nonchalance at first, then accelerating his retreat.

His face was clearly visible now; a surly, undistorted version of Monk Cado's. Dan reached for the door handle.

'Dan, they told us to stay here!'

'I don't think they saw him!'

But the detective across the street had; he was shouting to the officer at the apartment door and running toward Eddie Cado as Dan flung the car door open.

Cado looked over his shoulder as he neared the car, hearing the running footsteps; there were two men running in his direction now. Terror-stricken, he threw the paper bag aside. A carton of milk crumpled on the walk, splashing its contents. He hesitated a split second, his bulging eyes surveying the car, the wild possibility of using it for escape probably darting through his mind. He must have given up the thought as unfeasible, because he started to run again. Audrey screamed in the same instant that Dan Agnew lunged at him.

It was all compressed into one horrifying instant; Dan's attempt to stop Eddie Cado with a flying tackle that missed its mark, throwing Dan off balance. Dan sprawling on his stomach, half on the lawn, half on the sidewalk, but holding onto Eddie Cado's ankles with a strong grip.

Audrey heard herself scream once more as the stocky hoodlum reached into a trouser pocket to withdraw something that flashed blindingly in the sun, lifting it high in the air as he attempted to free himself from Dan's tenacious hold on his legs.

There only that instant in which the knife glittered in the sunlight as Eddie Cado flexed his knees and bent forward to plunge it into Dan's back. One speck of time in which someone yelled, 'Drop it!' and the scream reverberated once more in Audrey's throat, punctuating the sound of gunshots . . . one, two, then a third, exploding in the quiet summer afternoon with the impact of heavy artillery.

Eddie Cado's body jerked violently. His face contorted in a grimace of pain, and he seemed to tighten his grip on the knife handle, squeezing it hard in a momentary, frozen tableau. Then his fingers flew open as if someone had snapped a controlling spring, and the knife dropped to the sidewalk, clinking to the concrete only a half-breath before his limp form collapsed beside Dan.

Then there were officers swarming over the spot, gathering around the crumpled, bleeding shape on the walk. Dan was lumbering to his feet, breathing hard and moving slowly, a bewildered expression on his face. He may not even have known how close to death he had come; in his position he probably hadn't seen the poised knife.

One of the detectives who had driven them to Long Beach was slipping his gun back into its holster. Another bent over the prostrate body, reporting, 'He's dead.'

'Better let the doctor here check,' another said.

'It doesn't take a doctor to tell. He's had it. Not too soon, either.' Handkerchief in hand, the officer stooped to retrieve Eddie Cado's last weapon.

'I guess it . . . could have been me,' Dan was saying. 'I don't know what to . . .'

The detective whose gun had saved Dan's life sounded half-admiring, half-reproving as he said, 'That was a crazy thing to do, Doctor.'

Audrey opened the car door. Her legs trembled as she placed her weight on them, and for a moment she was afraid to move, convinced that her knees would buckle under her.

'Are you all right, miss?' One of the detectives was helping her out of the car.

'Yes. Yes, thank you.' She managed to reach Dan in spite of a gathering crowd; startled housewives and curious kids formed a second circle around Eddie Cado's body, ignoring police orders to stand back.

Audrey resisted an overwhelming impulse to throw her arms around Dan. She settled for clutching his forearm; grateful for the warm, live, flesh-and-blood reality beneath her fingers. 'Oh, Dan . . . Dan, that was too close!'

Dan took time to shake his head from side to side, reviving his dazed senses. 'Close doesn't count. Let's get over to the room.'

'All right, everybody, let's stand back please!' An officer was clearing an aisle on the sidewalk, helping Dan and Audrey push through the growing ring of morbid gawkers. Less venturesome neighbors stood in the apartment courtyards, examining Dan and Audrey curiously as they hurried toward the apartment Eddie Cado had selected for his hideout.

An ambulance pulled up in front of the stucco building as they entered the yard. Evidently one of the officers had been detailed to cover the rear of the building. He came running toward them now from a far end of the neglected tropical garden; a red-faced, puffy young man in a too-new uniform. 'Did they get him?'

'Yes. Get us inside this place!' Dan's edginess released itself in an angry shout. 'Hurry!'

The rookie tried the door. 'It's locked. One of the fellas will have a skeleton key, but doesn't look like there's anyone inside.' He started running toward the group near the car. 'Three shots. None of the officers got hurt?'

'No! Look, there's got to be a faster way!'

'Is there a back door?' Audrey asked. The delay was maddening, though no more than a minute or two had elapsed since the shooting.

An elderly, leather-tanned woman, stringy and freakish-looking in immodest white shorts and halter, came bristling from one of the apartments at the end of the row. An enormous ring of keys was draped over her bony wrist. 'You people with the police? I'm the manager here.'

Two of the detectives had left the scene of the shooting and arrived in time to convince the bronzed old harridan that Dan and

186

Audrey had no designs on her secondhand furniture.

'More racket around here!' she complained. 'Last night a buncha drunks in A-4, now all this.' She jangled the keys like an angry jailer. 'What's goin' on? Mr. Taylor get in some kind of trouble? Had enough, seems to me, his wife leavin' him an' the . . . girl.'

'Please!' Dan was breathing down her neck, his patience with the slow key-juggling process exhausted.

'All right . . . all right . . . it sticks sometimes.'

She's seen Bonnie, Audrey thought. *She's seen her alive!*

There was a clicking sound and a thud as the door was pushed open. Dan broke into the room first, Audrey close behind him, followed by the two detectives.

There was no one in the musty living room with its attached Pullman kitchen. But the couch was there: 'Eddie sleeps on the couch.' Dan shoved aside a dirty yellow rayon curtain. Monk had described it; the curtain closing off a small, dark bedroom in which the only window had been draped with what appeared to be a blanket.

Dan cursed softly. 'Can't see a thing in here!'

Audrey yanked at the window covering. It was a blanket, a cheap cotton blanket emblazoned with a brown-and-red Indian design.

It seemed incongruous to note this small detail as daylight blazed in to illuminate the room. Incongruous, because the next impression made any such trivial observations meaningless.

Bonnie Castle was lying diagonally across the bed, face down, motionless. If she had been capable of motion, she wouldn't have been able to travel far; her ankles were firmly bound by a length of new clothesline rope, one end secured to a brass post at the foot of the bed.

'The swine!' Dan's fury was matched only by the choking sensation in Audrey's throat.

'Is she sleeping, or is she? . . .'

Dan brushed the detective's anxious question aside with an order. 'Untie that. Go easy! Audrey, help me turn her. Just slightly. Someone get those ambulance attendants in here!'

Together they supported the child's body, moving her gently . . . and only slightly. The flesh of her arm felt cold to Audrey's touch. There was no visible sign of respiration, and Bonnie's pinched white face contrasted dishearteningly with a marked cyanosis of the lips—the blue-gray discoloration associated with shock and death.

There was a sickening stillness while Dan listened and touched, murmuring taciturn reports that held out no hope, yet continuing the prescribed tests with the terrible determination that drives a doctor or nurse to reject the admission of finality.

He knows she's dead. Audrey held the limp little wrist between her fingers, chilled by the lifeless weight. *He knows she's dead, but he won't believe it. When something is this cruelly wrong, you can't believe it!*

'God, I don't believe it!'

It was an unspoken prayer and a protest and an inward screaming at the injustice. A blasphemous prayer, perhaps, but it was life defying death, a demand that the innocent be blessed now that the guilty had been destroyed. Audrey blinked back the hot tears, but only for a moment. They were rolling across her face, blistering and unchecked, when she said it again. 'God, I don't believe it!'

In the same moment she was electrified by the faint, feeble throb under her fingertips. Dan must have caught that almost imperceptible pulse, too, because he was staring into Audrey's eyes, his own eyes lighted with a wild, almost fanatical light.

In another minute Bonnie Castle was being lifted, carefully and quickly, to a stretcher, and Dan was hurrying ahead of the attendants to make certain the oxygen would be ready as soon as she was eased into the ambulance.

One minute more and Audrey was beside him in the speeding ambulance, her sensitive fingers closed once more over Bonnie's fragile wrist, reaching occasionally to brush the damp black curls from the child's forehead.

'I'm getting a firmer pulse,' she said quietly.

With most of her tiny face covered by the oxygen mask, there was no way of determining if the blue color still haunted the child's lips, but her rhythmic breathing held a promise of resurrection.

'Thanks for not going to pieces,' Dan said fondly.

'Not yet. I will later.'

For the fourth time that day, they sped through the traffic with someone else at the wheel. For the second time, their urgent mission was announced by sirens.

'As soon as she's in good hands, I'm going to go to pieces like nothing you've ever seen before,' Audrey warned. She wished he weren't staring at her so intently. She couldn't remember when she had slept last, or washed her face, or applied lipstick, and she knew that the aching tiredness in her bones must be reflected in her eyes.

Then, suddenly aware that Dan himself wouldn't have passed any sartorial inspection, she was struck by the significance of his admiring expression. 'You look awful on the outside, Dr. Agnew,' she said softly. 'I guess I do, too.'

Dan nodded slowly. His eyes didn't leave her face, and it was obvious that he understood what she was saying. 'You look awfully good to me on the inside, Audrey. Where it matters.'

She would have told Dan, once again, that she loved him. But the ambulance was pulling into the emergency driveway of the Long Beach hospital, and Bonnie Castle had opened her eyes.

* * *

All the tensions that had accumulated since three o'clock that morning should have erupted as soon as Bonnie Castle was declared out of danger.

Ordinarily, without an hour-long crying jag to release the pent-up pressures, Audrey might have suffered severe emotional repercussions later. It was Dr. Agnew's order that circumvented the tearful collapse. And somehow the traumatic aftereffects never developed.

It was part of the fabric of dreams. Audrey was in a cool, restfully decorated hospital room, and a nurse who might have been Joanie Hazelrigg—except that her hair was three shades grayer and her uniform was two sizes larger—a wonderfully understanding, soft-spoken nurse was helping Audrey through the undreamed-of luxury of a hot bath, and massaging her back, and saying, 'Swallow these, honey. Doctor's orders. You'll be asleep in two minutes.' Audrey obeyed dutifully.

Crisp white hospital sheets and the firm, floating support of a genuine hospital bed! Audrey settled her head against the pillow. 'What's today?'

'Saturday,' the chubby angel in white said cheerfully. 'Why?'

Audrey sighed. 'I'm not on duty tonight. Isn't that lucky?'

'For you and for your patients,' the fat nurse said. No, the plump nurse. The chubby nurse. Oh, she was beginning to look better and better as Audrey's eyelids drooped! 'You're really beat out, dear. That doctor of yours was certainly worried about you.'

'He was?' Drowsily now.

'You've got yourself a guy there, honey. He'd be handsome, too, if you could talk him into getting his whites measured to fit. And what's he got against shaving?'

'Too busy,' Audrey muttered. 'He's been . . . too busy.' She closed her eyes.

'It takes all kinds,' the beautiful nurse said. And then Audrey heard the slim, lovely nurse who looked like Joanie Hazelrigg pad across the room, open the door, and close it behind her quietly, the way a proper nurse should.

Chapter 14

Two weeks had gone by since Audrey's fourteen-hour sleep at the Long Beach hospital. Now, in a fourth-floor room at Hollywood Memorial, she was wide-awake, though she had just put in an eight-hour tour of duty in O.R.—on the morning shift. Seven to three, those were the hours when important surgery was scheduled and important surgeons like Dr. Agnew demanded a scrub nurse who knew her business.

But this wasn't the O.R. It was three-fifteen, and her presence in Jeff Beaumont's room was purely social.

Jeff's bed was rolled up to an angle not unlike that of a patio lounge, a position that suited him admirably. He even managed to handle the glass of water in his hand with a casual sophistication that implied it was really a highball.

'Actually, aside from the dearth of good Scotch, I like it here,' Jeff was saying. 'Everybody who wants my autograph already has it. It was a drag for a few days, but now I'm John Citizen again. And my secretary says the fan mail's tripled since that little altercation with Vincent's stiletto. If my gut didn't hurt when I laugh, I'd say it was a classic publicity stunt.'

'You don't mean that,' Audrey said. 'You wouldn't be so flippant if you'd seen yourself when they brought you in. Brother!'

'Yeah, I guess I wasn't exactly an appealing sight.' Jeff sipped through the bent glass straw. 'Crazy booze they serve here. No hangover.' He leaned back against the propped pillows. 'Y'know, Red, it's a screwy world. Here I am, sitting on top of a world Roger Castle carved out for me. I'm supposed to hate the guy. You know what? I can't.'

'Is it because he tried to stop Vince?'

'From letting me have it? I dunno, Red. I don't remember that bit too clearly. First of all, I was carrying a heavy load. I remember this nut breaking into the room, and I remember Eddie Cado and Roger getting into a hassle about . . . oh-h, Eddie wanted to cut into the drug business and Roger couldn't see it. Eddie was really hung up for a fix. Desperate enough to try anything. And Roger reaches for the phone. I remember Eddie pulling the knife and Vince twisting it out of his hand. I just lay there, y'know? Like paralyzed! And the next thing that comes through, Eddie's zooming out the window like a bluebird, and Vince-baby's stuck with a knife and all this venom, and no target, y'see?'

'And, besides, you'd heard the whole history of Roger's heroin empire.'

'Uhuh. So there I am, and there's Vince, and there's Roger whimpering, "No, no . . .

194

he'll forget all about it—he's drunk. Don't do it!" But Roger isn't fast enough or forceful enough. And, like I noted to the gendarmes, baby . . . suddenly I go from feeling no pain to feeling all of it.'

'You're still lucky,' Audrey said. 'Here you are with your fan mail tripled. And where's Vince? Indicted for attempted murder. And Roger with him.'

Jeff stirred his innocent 'drink' with the glass straw contemplatingly. 'Sporting of you and Dan Agnew not to press kidnapping charges.'

'We couldn't, Jeff. He did that because of Bonnie. Roger may have been wrong, but it was part of the only decent instinct in him. Dan and I . . . well, let's say, we couldn't heap more hot coals on him because he loved somebody.'

'I'm digging you all the way,' Jeff droned. 'Love the guy where he deserves to be loved. Hate him for'—Jeff closed his eyes for a moment—'hate him for what he did to guys like my friend Buddy. Hate him for every talent, every kid that got hooked—just so Roger could throw his loot around on dames and parties.'

'A part of me,' Audrey said, 'can even hate him for what he did to a pathetic creature like Monk. Supplied him, denied him, and then, because he was stupid, fixed it so that Dan and I lied to him . . . Jeff, you're terribly fortunate.

195

You know that?'

'I've got it made.'

'Well, some morning when you're shaving that beautiful face of yours, ask yourself what it would be like to go through life looking like Eddie's kid brother.'

'I've only seen newspaper pictures,' Jeff admitted.

'Well, I've seen the real thing, Jeff. With all this fan mail you're getting, you're *really* sitting on top of the heap.'

'Get to the point, lover.'

'Dan can give you the name of a good plastic surgeon. You'll never miss the fee. Monk's back in jail, but there's no reason why somebody couldn't give him a break.'

'If I say it's done, will you spare me a further bath of tears?'

'You're spared.'

'It's done,' Jeff said.

Audrey got up to leave. 'I've got another visit to make.'

'Bonnie?'

'Yes. They brought her over from Long Beach yesterday. She's scheduled for an aortic commisurotomy tomorrow morning.'

'Chances?' Jeff was unusually solemn now.

'They can't be called good. I can only tell you who's operating. That should make a difference.'

'Big difference,' Jeff agreed.

Audrey walked to the door. 'I'd like to stay

for the full visiting hour, but I promised Bonnie . . .'

'It's okay, Red. Ginger's supposed to come by and help me kill until four o'clock.' He cradled his head in the folded pillow. 'Poor kid. Lost her father image. This bit with Roger really threw her. It's a tossup whether she comes in to cheer me up or vice versa.' Jeff smiled a smile familiar to millions, yet it seemed strangely personal to Audrey. 'How's the romance department, Red? Swingin' your way?'

Audrey shrugged her shoulders. 'Dan's available, but not exactly unattached.'

'Would I be paying back a big debt if I helped with the detachment? Ginger's ripe for a change. And who knows? We have a lot in common. We're both ambitious, useless, and lacking in character. We might deserve each other for a month or two.' Jeff grinned. 'Beat it, Red. I'm expecting a visitor.'

'You're a conceited idiot,' Audrey told him.

'Yes, but I'm lovable. And I'm never dull at parties.' Jeff was drinking from the water glass as though someone had spiked it with his favorite brand of Scotch. When he had drained its contents, he said, 'Anytime things get dull, I can always show the kids my scars. For *this*, honey, I owe you and the doc a few minor favors.'

Ginger Lampton was waiting in the fourth-floor reception room, but she wasn't alone.

'We've been waiting,' Dan told Audrey, not without annoyance. 'I should say *Ginger's* been waiting for her audience with his nibs.'

'I'm sorry if I stayed too long,' Audrey apologized.

Ginger was smiling at her. A warm, affectionate, unpatronizing, and only slightly phoney smile. She looked ravishing in a low-cut summer print of raw silk and an enormously wide-brimmed hat that somehow failed to accentuate her full-blown figure. 'I don't want to rush anybody, Miss West, but I'm dying to tell Jeff about my new manager. Pete Carlisle. I was lost, absolutely lost, when this horrible mess with Roger came up, but Petey's made everything sane and sensible and sweet again. You know? And Jeff's going to be facing the same dreadful problems, poor baby —no one to look after all those maddening details like money, money, money.'

'He'll suffer,' Audrey agreed. 'He was just telling me, he needs somebody who cares.'

Dan shot Audrey a withering glance. She was managing, deliberately, to sound as shallow and frivolous as Ginger Lampton.

'Did he actually say that? Poor angel: that ghastly experience, and now no one to look after him.' Ginger leaped up from the plastic settee she had been occupying. 'You've got to excuse me, lambs. When I think of that miserable darling all alone in that dingy room . . . and all Petey could do for him . . .'

Ginger was on her way to the corridor that led to Jeff's room when she turned to beam her most enchanting smile at Dan. Her voice was never in better form. Throaty, sexy, deep. She let it ooze from her throat, the words as honeyed and meaningless as the lyrics she would pour out to a Sunset Strip audience before the night was over. 'Call me when you have a free afternoon, sweetie. Anytime you're lunchish.'

Dan was laughing quietly when Ginger turned the corner and disappeared from sight.

'Something's funny?' Audrey asked.

'No, it's mysterious. Who will replace young Doctor Agnew on her calendar? Jeff-baby, or Petey-sweetie?'

Audrey laughed, too. 'I couldn't tell. I know Jeff's going to be in there trying. But let's not underestimate the new dark horse.'

'Let's just be glad she kissed off the jackass,' Dan said. He sounded contrite and foolish, but when he escorted Audrey to Bonnie Castle's room on the third floor, he was anything but the rejected lover. 'One thing we know,' he said gleefully. 'It's not going to be me!'

*   *   *

'Today my *daddy's* coming,' Bonnie Castle said. Her breath was short, and there was a general weakness about her movements on

199

the high hospital bed, but she was smiling that shy, engaging smile that had endeared her not only to Audrey, but to all of the third-floor staff.

'I don't know, honey.' Audrey wondered who had given the curly-haired child such an impossible impression. 'Your daddy's very busy, you know. Maybe he can't come today.'

'Dr. Dan said he will. He wouldn't fool me.'

Audrey kissed the little girl's cheek, remembering the frightening ordeal in that musty Long Beach apartment. 'You like Dr. Dan, don't you?'

'He's going to make me all better tomorrow. In the morning,' Bonnie said. 'I have to go to sleep early, because he's coming real, real early.'

'And he told you your daddy? . . .'

'At half pas' three o'clock,' Bonnie said eagerly. Her eyes shone with the expectation.

It was nearly four. Dan should have known better than to raise the child's hopes—not even to pacify her during a tearful fit of loneliness, Audrey thought. Roger's entire battery of attorneys hadn't managed to free him on bail, and the chances of a visit from him were extremely slim.

Unless someone convinced the police department that a visit from him would be invaluable to the morale of a little girl who would face death tomorrow morning, as she had faced it twice before . . .

It must have been this effort on Dan's part that made Bonnie Castle's innocently assumed visit from her father a reality.

Roger came into the room as Audrey was preparing to leave. He didn't come alone. The plainclothesman who accompanied him may have had a daughter of his own. At any rate, he made it a point to keep his right arm lowered and to stand just a shade behind his charge. From her perch on the high bed, Bonnie couldn't possibly see that Roger Castle and the stranger who accompanied him were handcuffed together.

Roger nodded politely to Audrey. It was as though she had never been a guest in his home—once by invitation, once by gunpoint.

'Daddy . . . *Daddy!* I *said* you were going to come!'

'Easy, honey!' Roger kissed his daughter's cheek, speaking softly in an effort to keep her calm.

'Are you going to stay? Dr. Dan said you're going to be right outside the door when I get my operation. It's in the morning.'

Roger's free hand was petting the tiny face. 'Oh, you know I'm gonna be here, honey. Sure thing. An' after that, you gotta get all better, right? So you're gonna go stay with Auntie Claire. You never seen your Auntie Claire, but, see, she's Daddy's sister. You get it? She's a swell gal—lives up in Santa Barbara, so she's gonna take you t' the beach, an' she got this little girl just about your own age . . .'

'I want *you* to come, too, Daddy.'

'Oh, I'll come. Sure! You think I wouldn't? Heck, I only got this little . . . business deal I gotta take care of, an' then you an' me, we're gonna . . .'

Audrey tiptoed toward the door, hoping to escape the room before Roger's unbelievable reserve broke down completely. *Because he knew! He knew through every childish question and every agonizing reply that he might not see Bonnie again. Even if she survived the operation tomorrow, he might not see her again!*

Childlike, Bonnie changed the subject abruptly. 'Who's that man?'

'This man?' Audrey turned to see Roger force a delighted smile. 'Why, this is a friend of Daddy's, honey. Carl. Bonnie, meet Carl. Carl, meet Bonnie.'

Solemnly, the little girl said, 'How d'you do?'

'I'm very happy to know you, Bonnie,' Carl said. Maybe his name was Joe or Fred or Harry, but he was playing 'Friend Carl' to the hilt. 'Your daddy said he wanted me to meet you.'

'I sure did!' Roger's enthusiasm was heartbreaking. 'Listen, when I told Carl about you, he said, "How 'bout we bring Bonnie a nice present?" You got it there, Carl? That present you got Bonnie?'

Kingpin hoodlum and stoic-faced cop. They

were watching Bonnie unwrap a lady doll garbed in a lacey white wedding gown when Audrey West hurried out of the room.

She was with Dr. Dan Agnew when Roger Castle and his guard came through the waiting room.

'I'd like t' say thanks, Doc,' Roger said tonelessly.

'For crossing you up with that fake operation on Monk?' Dan accepted Roger's extended hand, but they averted each other's eyes.

'Skip that. You got 'er back *your* way. It don't matter if I was right or you had it figured better. You got 'er back.'

'We both wanted that, Roger.'

'Yeah. Well, I thought I'd say that.'

Carl shifted from one foot to the other uncomfortably. 'I'm gonna be outta circulation, but I got a sister up north—she called me, an' it's o.k. with her an' her husband. The kid's got a good place t' go. This guy's a schoolteacher. Hasn't got a dime, but I got a couple policies the cops can't touch, so the kid won't have no worries. You follow me? So she fergets about the ole man—ten, twenny years. So what? A guy can't have everything. Know what I mean, Doc?'

'I know what you mean,' Dan said.

'Get this, Doc. I'm not givin' you no pat on the back fer crossin' me, pal. Puttin' the finger on a guy that tried t' give you a break. I just 'preciate the visit with the kid. I mean, you fixed it up. O.K., so I'll be waiting' fer a call tomorrow, see? *You* do the job—don't ring in no crummy quack, see? She gets the best!'

'My best,' Dan promised.

Roger had humiliated himself long enough. He puffed out his chest and pointed at Dan, the diamond on his finger flashing under the electric lights. 'You do a good job, you'll get taken care of. Know what I mean?'

Dan knew what he meant, and so did Audrey. What they would never know was why a man capable of a love so deep that he was actually hoping a tiny six-year-old would live to forget him completely . . . why a man like that had trafficked in a commodity with only one use—to destroy other loves and other lives.

And seeing him walk to the elevators, wrist-to-wrist with his jailer, Audrey pondered on the irony that had brought Roger Castle to the end of the line.

Drugs had made him a king. A drug had saved his child's life. And the same drug had written his demise. Somewhere between heroin and sodium amytal, Roger Castle's world had crumbled.

*   *   *

Exactly three days and five hours later, Charlie Perkins raised his glass and proposed a toast. 'To the happy couple. And congratulations upon the success of Dr. Agnew's most trying operation!'

There were six of them seated around the table in the duplex apartment: Joan Hazelrigg and her new beau (two-hundred and fifty pounds of placid-face lab technician named Larry Bean), Irene Rafferty and Charlie Perkins, who had thoughtfully arranged the celebration, and, of course, the guests of honor, Dan and Audrey.

Audrey's friends went through the clinking routine gaily, and gulped from the champagne glasses. Larry winced after the first taste.

'Guava juice. Isn't it exotic?' Irene was playing her hostess role to the hilt—a skinny Elsa Maxwell in a brand new Hawaiian print wraparound, this one featuring stylized creatures of the deep.

Joanie's boy friend agreed that guava juice was indeed exotic, and was thereupon told its vitamin content by Charlie Perkins.

Irene beamed. Joanie surveyed the dinner laid out before her and attempted to beam. She had a new boy friend at stake, and chances were he hadn't been prepared for yogurt, dates, macadamia nuts, and cookies made from what appeared to be kelp and ground cornstalks. Mr. Bean looked like a meat-and-potatoes man. When he didn't think anyone was watching him, he also looked miserable.

They discussed Bonnie Castle and the hopeful result of her operation; with sympathetic and straight-living relatives, her chances of leading a reasonably normal life had been greatly enhanced. Dr. Dan hadn't failed her, and Audrey had been at his side, wishing Dr. Voss could have watched the operation, too.

After that, while Irene plied them with ice cream made from goat's milk and organically grown blueberries, there was an animated discussion about where Dan and Audrey should spend their honeymoon. There was going to be a simple ceremony next Saturday, after which Charlie recommended a marvelous health resort that featured a diet of undiluted grape juice and wheat germ. Larry Bean thought a cabin in the Sierras would be better, and Joanie chimed in to say that she loved cabins in the Sierras, especially for people who didn't want to be bothered by other people.

Joan and her boy friend left soon after dinner, probably headed for the most convenient steak house. Considerately, Charlie and Irene did the dishes and remembered a health lecture that they couldn't bear to miss.

When the door had closed behind their dinner-party hosts, Dan wasted no time in sweeping Audrey into his arms.

'Thanks,' she told him. 'For being so

patient.'

'Patient?'

'You were a polite angel. I actually think Irene's getting fond of you.'

'Love me, love my roommate. Is that what you're trying to get across?' Dan kissed Audrey's forehead and then her cheek. 'Irene and I buried the hatchet tonight. Anyway, she's not going to be your roommate after Saturday.'

'I know, darling.'

'So I could afford to be polite.'

'But you're probably starved.'

'That's a good word for it,' Dan said. He kissed her again, less brotherly this time. 'I've been starved for a long time. I've been wandering around in the woods, looking for you.'

Audrey buried her head against the warm strength of his shoulder. 'Stop looking, Doctor,' she said quietly. 'Just hold me close and stop looking.'